ALSO BY *E. L. Doctorow*

E. L. DOCTOROW is an award-winning author whose work is published in over thirty languages. His novels include *Welcome to Hard Times*, *The Book of Daniel*, *Ragtime*, *Loon Lake*, *World's Fair*, *Billy Bathgate*, *City of God* and *The March*. He has published two short story collections, *Lives of the Poets* and *Sweet Land Stories*, and three volumes of essays, the most recent of which is *Creationists*. Among his honours are the National Book Award, three National Book Critics Circle awards, two PEN/Faulkner awards, the Edith Wharton Citation for Fiction, the William Dean Howells Medal of the American Academy of Arts and Letters and the presidentially conferred National Humanities Medal. He lives in New York.

'A book more moving and more haunting than anything he has done before' *London Review of Books*

'E.L. Doctorow's beguiling eleventh novel curates the basic facts of the Collyer history . . . American history knocks noisily at the door and its emissaries drift in and out' *Guardian*

'An extraordinary picaresque tale of New York's material evolution and entropic decay' *The Times*

'A sad and beautiful story of the love of two brothers rejected by the rest of the world' *New Statesman*

E. L. DOCTOROW

HOMER
AND
LANGLEY

ABACUS

First published in Great Britain in 2009 by Little, Brown
This paperback edition published in 2011 by Abacus
Reprinted 2011, 2012

A CIP catalogue record for this book
is available from the British Library.

ISBN 978-0-349-12259-5

Printed and bound in Great Britain by
Clays Ltd, St Ives plc

Papers used by Abacus are from well-managed forests
and other responsible sources.

MIX
Paper from
responsible sources
FSC   FSC® C104740
www.fsc.org

Abacus
An imprint of
Little, Brown Book Group
100 Victoria Embankment
London EC4Y 0DY

An Hachette UK Company
www.hachette.co.uk

www.littlebrown.co.uk

To Kate Medina

HOMER & LANGLEY

I'M HOMER, THE BLIND BROTHER. I DIDN'T LOSE MY SIGHT all at once, it was like the movies, a slow fade-out. When I was told what was happening I was interested to measure it, I was in my late teens then, keen on everything. What I did this particular winter was to stand back from the lake in Central Park where they did all their ice skating and see what I could see and couldn't see as a day-by-day thing. The houses over to Central Park West went first, they got darker as if dissolving into the dark sky until I couldn't make them out, and then the trees began to lose their shape, and then finally, this was toward the end of the season, maybe it was late February of that very cold winter, and all I could see were these phantom shapes of the ice skaters floating past me on a field of ice, and then the white ice, that last light, went gray and then altogether black, and then all my sight was gone though I could hear clearly the scoot scut of the blades on the ice, a very satisfying sound, a soft sound though full of intention, a deeper tone than you'd expect made by the skate blades, perhaps for having sounded the resonant basso of the water under the ice, scoot scut, scoot scut. I would hear someone going someplace fast, and then the twirl into that long scurratch as the skater spun to a stop, and then I laughed too for the joy of that ability of the skater to come to a dead stop all at once, going along scoot scut and then scurratch.

Of course I was sad too, but it was lucky this happened to me when I was so young with no idea of being disabled, moving on in my mind to my other capacities like my exceptional hearing, which I trained to a degree of alertness that was almost visual. Langley said I had ears like a bat and he tested that proposition, as he liked to subject everything to review. I was of course familiar with our house, all four storeys of it, and could navigate every room and up and down the stairs without hesitation, knowing where everything was by memory. I knew the drawing room, our father's study, our mother's sitting room, the dining room with its eighteen chairs and the walnut long table, the butler's pantry and the kitchens, the parlor, the bedrooms, I remembered how many of the carpeted steps there were between the floors, I didn't even have to hold on to the railing, you could watch me and if you didn't know me you wouldn't know my eyes were dead. But Langley said the true test of my hearing capacity would come when no memory was involved, so he shifted things around a bit, taking me into the music room, where he had earlier rolled the grand piano around to a different corner and had put the Japanese folding screen with the herons in water in the middle of the room, and for good measure twirled me around in the doorway till my entire sense of direction was obliterated, and I had to laugh because don't you know I walked right around that folding screen and sat down at the piano exactly as if I knew where he had put it, as I did, I could hear surfaces, and I said to Langley, A blind bat whistles, that's the way he does it, but I didn't have to whistle, did I? He was truly amazed, Langley is the older of us by two years, and I have always liked to impress him in whatever way I could. At this time he was already a college student in his first year at Columbia. How do you do it? he said. This is of scientific interest. I said: I feel shapes as they push the air away, or I feel heat from things, you can turn me around till I'm dizzy, but I can still tell where the air is filled in with something solid.

And there were other compensations as well. I had tutors for my education and then, of course, I was comfortably enrolled in the West End Conservatory of Music, where I had been a student since my sighted years. My skill as a pianist rendered my blindness acceptable in the social world. As I grew older, people spoke of my gallantry, and the girls certainly liked me. In our New York society of those days, one parental means of ensuring a daughter's marriage to a suitable husband was to warn her, from birth it seemed, to watch out for men and to not quite trust them. This was well before the Great War, when the days of the flapper and women smoking cigarettes and drinking martinis were in the unimaginable future. So a handsome young blind man of reputable family was particularly attractive insofar as he could not, even in secret, do anything untoward. His helplessness was very alluring to a woman trained since birth, herself, to be helpless. It made her feel strong, in command, it could bring out her sense of pity, it could do lots of things, my sightlessness. She could express herself, give herself to her pent-up feelings, as she could not safely do with a normal fellow. I dressed very well, I could shave myself with my straight razor and never nick the skin, and at my instructions the barber kept my hair a bit longer than it was being worn in that day, so that when at some gathering I sat at the piano and played the

Appassionata, for instance, or the Revolutionary Étude, my hair would fly about—I had a lot of it then, a good thick mop of brown hair parted in the middle and coming down each side of my head. Franz Lisztian hair is what it was. And if we were sitting on a sofa and no one was about, a young lady friend might kiss me, touch my face and kiss me, and I, being blind, could put my hand on her thigh without seeming to have that intention, and so she might gasp, but would leave it there for fear of embarrassing me.

I should say that as a man who never married I have been particularly sensitive to women, very appreciative in fact, and let me admit right off that I had a sexual experience or two in this time I am describing, this time of my blind city life as a handsome young fellow not yet twenty, when our parents were still alive and had many soirees, and entertained the very best people of the city in our home, a monumental tribute to late Victorian design that would be bypassed by modernity—as for instance the interior fashions of our family friend Elsie de Wolfe, who, after my father wouldn't allow her to revamp the entire place, never again set foot in our manse—and which I always found comfortable, solid, dependable, with its big upholstered pieces, or tufted Empire side chairs, or heavy drapes over the curtains on the ceiling-to-floor windows, or medieval tapestries hung from gilt poles, and bow-windowed bookcases, thick Persian rugs, and standing lamps with tasseled shades and matching chinois amphora that you could almost step into . . . it was all very eclectic, being a record of sorts of our parents' travels, and cluttered it might have seemed to outsiders, but it seemed normal and right to us and it was our legacy, Langley's and mine, this sense of living with things assertively inanimate, and having to walk around them.

Our parents went abroad for a month every year, sailing away on one ocean liner or another, waving from the railing of some great three- or four-stacker—the *Carmania*? the *Mauretania*? the *Neuresthania*?—as she pulled away from the dock. They looked so small up there, as small as I felt with my hand in the tight hand of my nurse, and the ship's horn sounding in my feet and the gulls flying about as if in celebration, as if something really fine was going on. I used to wonder what would happen to my father's patients while he was away, for he was a prominent women's doctor and I worried that they would get sick and maybe die, waiting for him to return.

Even as my parents were running around England, or Italy, or Greece or Egypt, or wherever they were, their return was presaged by things in crates delivered to the back door by the Railway Express Company: ancient Islamic tiles, or rare books, or a marble water fountain, or busts of Romans with no noses or missing ears, or antique armoires with their fecal smell.

And then, finally, with great huzzahs, there, after I'd almost forgotten all about them, would be Mother and Father themselves stepping out of the cab in front of our house, and carrying in their arms such treasures as hadn't preceded them. They were not entirely thoughtless parents for there were always presents for Langley and me, things to really excite a boy, like an antique toy train that was too delicate to play with, or a gold-plated hairbrush.

—

WE DID SOME TRAVELING as well, my brother and I, being habitual summer campers in our youth. Our camp was in Maine on a coastal plateau of woods and fields, a good place to appreciate Nature. The more our country lay under blankets of factory smoke, the more the coal came rattling up from the mines, the more our massive locomotives thundered through the night and big harvesting machines sliced their way through the crops and black cars filled the streets, blowing their horns and crashing into one another, the more the American people worshipped Nature. Most often this devotion was relegated to the children. So there we were living in primitive cabins in Maine, boys and girls in adjoining camps.

I was in the fullness of my senses, then. My legs were limber and my arms strong and sinewy and I could see the world with all the unconscious happiness of a fourteen-year-old. Not far from the camps, on a bluff overlooking the ocean, was a meadow profuse with wild blackberry bushes, and one afternoon numbers of us were there plucking the ripe blackberries and biting into their wet warm pericarped pulp, competing with flights of bumblebees, as we raced them from one bush to another and stuffed the berries into our mouths till the juice dripped down our chins. The air was thickened with floating communities of gnats that rose and fell, expanding and contracting, like astronomical events. And the sun shone on our heads, and behind us at the foot of the cliff were the black and silver rocks patiently taking and breaking apart the waves and, beyond that, the glittering sea radiant with shards of sun, and all of it in my clear eyes as I turned in triumph to this one girl with whom I had bonded, Eleanor was her name, and stretched my arms wide and bowed as the magician who had made it for her. And somehow when the others moved on we lingered conspiratorially behind a thicket of blackberry bushes until the sound of them was gone and we were there unattended, having broken camp rules, and so self-defined as more grown-up than anyone believed, though we grew reflective walking back, holding hands without even realizing it.

Is there any love purer than this, when you don't even know what it is? She had a moist warm hand, and dark eyes and hair, this Eleanor. Neither of us was embarrassed by the fact that she was a good head taller than me. I remember her lisp, the way her tongue tip was caught between her teeth when she pronounced her S's. She was not one of the socially self-assured ones who abounded in the girls' side of the camp. She wore the uniform green shirt and gray bloomers they all wore but she was something of a loner, and in my eyes she seemed distinguished, fetching, thoughtful, and in some state of longing analogous to my own—for what, neither of us could have said. This was my first declared affection and so serious that even Langley, who lived in another cabin with his age group, did not tease me. I wove a lanyard for Eleanor and cut and stitched a model birch bark canoe for her.

Oh, but this is a sad tale I have wandered into. The boys' and girls' camps were separated by a stand of woods through the length of which was a tall wire fence of the kind to keep animals out and so it was a major escapade at night for the older boys to climb over or dig under this fence and challenge authority by running through the girls' camp shouting and dodging pursuing counselors, and banging on cabin doors so as to elicit delighted shrieks. But Eleanor and I breached the fence to meet after everyone was asleep and to wander about under the stars and talk philosophically about life. And that's how it happened that on one warm August night we found ourselves down the road a mile or so at a lodge dedicated like our camp to getting back to nature. But it was for adults, for parents. Attracted by a flickering light in the otherwise dark manse we tiptoed up on the porch and through the window saw a shocking thing, what in later time would be called a blue movie. Its licentious demonstration was taking place on a portable screen something like a large window shade. In the reflected light we could see in silhouette an audience of attentive adults leaning forward in their chairs and sofas. I remember the sound of the projector not that far from the open window, the whirring sound it made, like a field of cicadas. The woman on the screen, naked but for a pair of high-heeled shoes, lay on her back on a table and the man, also naked, stood holding her legs under the knees so that she was proffered to receive his organ, of which he made sure first to exhibit its enormity to his audience. He was an ugly bald skinny man with just that one disproportionate feature to distinguish him. As he shoved himself again and again into the woman she was given to pulling her hair while her legs kicked up convulsively, each shoe tip jabbing the air in rapid succession, as if she'd been jolted with an electric current. I was rapt—

horrified, but also thrilled to a level of unnatural feeling that was akin to nausea. I do not wonder now that with the invention of moving pictures, their pornographic possibilities were immediately understood.

Did my friend gasp, did she tug at my hand to pull me away? If she did I would not have noticed. But when I was sufficiently recovered in my senses I turned and she was nowhere to be seen. I ran back the way we had come, and on this moonlit night, a night as black and white as the film, I could see no one on the road ahead of me. The summer had some weeks to go but my friend Eleanor never spoke to me again, or even looked my way, a decision I accepted as an accomplice, by gender, of the male performer. She was right to run from me, for on that night romance was unseated in my mind and in its place was enthroned the idea that sex was something you did to them, to all of them including poor shy tall Eleanor. It is a puerile illusion, hardly worthy of a fourteen-year-old mind, yet it persists among grown men even as they meet women more avidly copulative than they.

Of course part of me watching that tawdry little film felt no less betrayed by the adult world than did my Eleanor. I don't mean to imply that my mother and father were among that audience—they weren't. In fact when I confided in Langley, we agreed that our father and mother were exempt from the race of the carnally afflicted. We were not so childish as to think our parents indulged in sex merely the two times it took to conceive us. But it was a propriety of their generation that love was practiced in the dark and never mentioned or acknowledged at any other time. Life was made tolerable by its formalities. Even the most intimate relationships were addressed in formal terms. Our father was never without his fresh collar and tie and vested suit, I simply don't remember him dressed any other way. His steel gray hair was cut short, and he wore a brush mustache and pince-nez quite unaware that he was aping the look of the then president. And our mother, with her ample figure girdled in the style of that day, with her abundant hair swept up and pinned cornucopically, was a figure of matronly abundance. The women of her generation wore their skirts to the ankles. They did not have the vote, a fact that my mother found not at all disturbing, though some of her friends were suffragettes. Langley said about our parents that their marriage was made in Heaven. He meant by this not a great romance, but that our mother and father in their youth had conformed their lives dutifully to biblical specifications.

People my age are supposed to remember times long past though they can't recall what happened yesterday. My memories of our long-dead parents are considerably dimmed, as if having fallen further and further back in time has made them smaller, with less visible detail as if time has become space, become distance, and figures from the past, even your father and mother, are too far away to be recognized. They are fixed in their own time, which has rolled down behind the planetary horizon. They and their times and all its concerns have gone down together. I can remember a girl I knew slightly, like that Eleanor, but of my parents, for instance, I remember not one word that either of them ever said.

—

WHICH BRINGS ME to Langley's Theory of Replacements.

When it was first expounded I'm not sure, though I remember thinking there was something collegiate about it.

I have a theory, he said to me. Everything in life gets replaced. We are our parents' replacements just as they were replacements of the previous generation. All these herds of bison they are slaughtering out west, you would think that was the end of them, but they won't all be slaughtered and the herds will fill back in with replacements that will be indistinguishable from the ones slaughtered.

I said, Langley, people aren't all the same like dumb bison, we are each a person. A genius like Beethoven cannot be replaced.

But, you see, Homer, Beethoven was a genius for his time. We have the notations of his genius but he is not our genius. We will have our geniuses, and if not in music then in science or art, though it may take a while to recognize them because geniuses are usually not recognized right away. Besides, it's not what any of them achieve but how they stand in relation to the rest of us. Who is your favorite baseballer? he said.

Walter Johnson, I said.

And what is he if not a replacement for Cannonball Titcomb, Langley said. You see? It's social constructions I'm talking about. One of the constructions is for us to have athletes to admire, to create ourselves as an audience of admirers for baseballers. This seems to be a means of cultural communizing that creates great social satisfaction and possibly ritualizes, what with baseball teams of different towns, our tendency to murder one another. Human beings are not bison, we are a more complex species, living in complicated social constructions, but we replace ourselves just as they do. There will always be in America for as long as baseball is played someone who serves youth still to be born as Walter Johnson serves you. It is a legacy of ours to have baseball heroes and so there will always be one.

Well you are saying everything is always the same as if there is no progress, I said.

I'm not saying there's no progress. There is progress while at the same time nothing changes. People make things like automobiles, discover things like radio waves. Of course they do. There will be better pitchers than your Walter Johnson, as hard as that is to believe. But time is something else than what I'm talking about. It advances through us as we replace ourselves to fill the slots.

By this time I knew Langley's theory was something he was making up as he went along. What slots? I said.

Why are you too thick in the head to understand this? The slots for geniuses, and baseballers and millionaires and kings.

Is there a slot for blind people? I said. I was remembering, just as I said that, the way the eye doctor I'd been taken to shined a light in my eyes and muttered something in Latin as if the English language had no words for the awfulness of my fate.

For the blind, yes, and for the deaf, and for King Leopold's slaves in the Congo, Langley said.

In the next few minutes I had to listen carefully to see if he was still in the room because he had stopped talking. Then I felt his hand on my shoulder. At which point I understood that what Langley called his Theory of Replacements was his bitterness of life or despair of it.

Langley, I remember saying, your theory needs more work. Apparently he thought so too, for it was at this time that he began to save the daily newspapers.

IT WAS MY BROTHER, not either of my parents, who was in the habit of reading to me once I could no longer read for myself. Of course I had my books in Braille. I read all of Gibbon in Braille. *In the second century of the Christian era, the Empire of Rome comprehended the fairest part of the earth, and the most civilized portion of mankind* . . . I still believe that is a sentence more deliciously felt with one's fingers than seen with one's eyes. Langley read aloud to me from the popular books of the day— Jack London's *The Iron Heel,* and his stories of the Far North, or A. Conan Doyle's *The Valley of Fear,* about Sherlock Holmes and the fiendish Moriarty—but before he switched to newspapers, reading to me of the war in Europe to which he was destined to go, Langley used to bring back from the secondhand bookshops slim volumes of poetry and read from them as if poems were news. Poems have ideas, he said. The ideas of poems come out of their emotions and their emotions are carried on images. That makes poems far more interesting than your novels, Homer. Which are only stories.

I don't remember the names of the poets Langley found so

newsworthy, nor did the poems stick in my mind but for a line or two. But they pop up in my thoughts usually unbidden and they give me pleasure when I recite them to myself. Like *Generations have trod, have trod, have trod / And all is seared with trade, bleared, smeared with toil* . . .—there's a Langleyan idea for you.

WHEN HE WAS GOING off to war, my parents had a dinner for him, just the family at table—a good roast of beef, and the smell of candle wax and my mother weeping and apologizing for weeping and my father clearing his throat as he proposed a toast. Langley was to embark that night. Our soldier in the family was going over there to take the place of a dead Allied soldier, just according to his theory. At the front door I felt his face to memorize it at that moment, a long straight nose, a mouth set grimly, a pointed chin, much like my own, and then the overseas cap in his hand, and the rough cloth of his uniform, and the puttees on his legs. He had skinny legs, Langley. He stood straight and tall, taller and straighter than he would ever be again.

So there I was—without my brother for the first time in my life. I found myself as if vaulted into my own young independent manhood. That would be tested soon enough because of the Spanish flu pandemic that hit the city in 1918 and like some great predatory bird swooped down and took off both our parents. My father died first because he was associated with the Bellevue Hospital and that's where he came down with it. Naturally, my mother soon followed. I call them my father and mother when I think of them dying so suddenly and painfully, choking to death in a matter of hours, which is the way the Spanish flu did people in.

To this day I don't like to think about their deaths. It is true that with the onset of my blindness there had been a kind of a retrenchment of whatever feelings they had for me, as if an investment they had made had not paid off and they were cutting their losses. Nevertheless, nevertheless, this was the final abandonment, a trip from which they were not to return, and I was shaken.

It was said that the Spanish flu was taking mostly young people though in our case it was the opposite. I was spared though I did feel poorly for a while. I had to handle the arrangements for Mother as she had handled them for her husband before she too went and died, as if she couldn't bear to be away from him for a moment. I went to the same mortician she had used. Burying people was a roaring business at this time, the usual unctuous formalities were dispensed with and corpses were transported speedily to their graves by men whose muffled voices led me to understand they were wearing gauze masks. Prices had risen too: by the time Mother died the exact same arrangements she had made for Father cost double. They had had many friends, a large social circle, but only one or two distant cousins turned up for the obsequies, everyone else sitting home behind locked doors or going on to their own funerals. My parents are together for eternity at the Woodlawn Cemetery up past what was the village of Fordham, though it is all the Bronx now, and of course unless there's an earthquake.

At this time of the flu, Langley, gone to war in Europe with the AEF, was reported missing. An army officer had come to the door to deliver the news. Are you sure? I said. How do you know? Is this your way of saying he's been killed? No? Then you are not saying anything more than that you don't know anything. So why are you here?

Of course I had acted badly. I remember I had to calm myself by going to my father's whiskey cabinet and taking a slug of something right from the bottle. I asked myself if it was possible for my entire family to be wiped out in the space of a month or two. I decided it was not possible. It was not like my brother to desert me. There was something about Langley's worldview, firmly in place at his birth, though perhaps polished to a shine at Columbia College, that would confer godlike immunity to such an ordinary fate as death in a war: it was innocents who died, not those born with the strength of no illusions.

So once I persuaded myself of that, whatever state I was in, it was nothing like a mourning state. I was not grieving, I was waiting.

And then of course, through the slot in the front door, a letter from my brother from a hospital in Paris dated a week after I had received the official visit telling me he was missing in action. I had Siobhan our maid read the letter to me. Langley had been gassed on the western front. Nothing fatal, he said, and with certain compensations from attentive army nurses. When they tired of him, he said, he would be sent home.

Siobhan, a pious Irishwoman of a certain age, did not like to read of the attentions of army nurses, but I was laughing with relief and so she relented and had to admit how happy she was that Mr. Langley was alive and sounding just like himself.

UNTIL MY BROTHER got home, there I was alone in the house but for the staff, a butler, a cook, and two maids, all of whom had rooms and one bath on the top floor. You will ask how a blind man handles his business affairs with servants in the house who might think how easy it would be to steal something. It was the butler I worried about, not that he had actually done anything. But he was too slyly solicitous of me, now that I was in charge and no longer the son. So I fired him and kept the cook and the two maids, Siobhan and the younger Hungarian girl Julia, who smelled of almonds and whom I eventually took to bed. Actually he was not just a butler, Wolf, but a butler-chauffeur and sometime handyman. And when we still had a carriage he would bring it around from the stable on Ninety-third street and drive my father to the hospital at the crack of dawn. My father had been very fond of him. But he was a German, this Wolf, and while his accent was slight he could not put his verbs anywhere but at the end of the sentence. I had never forgiven him for the way he whipped our carriage horse, Jack, than whom no finer or more gallant a steed has ever lived, and though he had been in the family's employ since I could remember, Wolf, I mean, and while I could tell from his footsteps that he was no longer the youngest of men, we were, after all, at war with the Germans and so I fired him. He told me he knew that was the reason though I of course denied it. I said to him,

What is Wolf short for? Wolfgang, he said. Yes, I said, and that is why I'm firing you because you have no right to the name of the greatest genius in the history of music.

Even though I was giving him a nice packet of send-off money, he had the ill grace to curse me and leave by the front door, which he slammed for good measure.

But as I say it took some working out to settle my father's estate with his lawyers and to arrange some means of dealing with boring household management. I enlisted one of the junior clerks at the family bank to do the bookkeeping and once a week I put on a suit and slapped a derby on my head and set off down Fifth Avenue to the Corn Exchange. It was a good walk. I used a stick but really didn't need it having made a practice as soon as I knew my eyes were fading of surveying and storing in my memory everything for twenty blocks south and north, and as far east as First Avenue and to the paths in the park across the street all the way to Central Park West. I knew the length of the blocks by the number of steps it took from curb to curb. I was just as happy not to have to see the embarrassing Renaissance mansions of the robber barons to the south of us. I was a vigorous walker and gauged the progress of our times by the changing sounds and smells of the streets. In the past the carriages and the equipages hissed or squeaked or groaned, the drays rattled, the beer wagons pulled by teams passed thunderously, and the beat behind all this music was the clopping of the hooves. Then the combustive put-put of the motorcars was added to the mix and gradually the air lost its organic smell of hide and leather, the odor of horse manure on hot days did not hang like a miasma over the street nor did one now often hear that wide-pan shovel of the street cleaners shlushing it up, and eventually, at this particular time I am describing, it was all mechanical, the noise, as fleets of cars sailed past in both directions, horns tooting and policemen blowing their whistles.

I liked the nice sharp sound of my stick on the granite steps of the bank. And inside I sensed the architecture of high ceilings and marble walls and pillars from the hollowed-out murmur of voices and the chill on my ears. These were the days I thought I was acting responsibly, carrying on as a replacement of the previous Collyers as if I was hoping for their posthumous approval. And then Langley came home from the World War and I realized how foolish I had been.

DESPITE THE ASSURANCES of his letter, my brother returned was a different man. His voice was a kind of gargle and he kept coughing and clearing his throat. He had been a clear tenor when he left, and would sing the old arias as I played them. Not now. I felt his face and the hollowness of his cheeks and the sharpness of his cheekbones. And he had scars. When he removed his uniform I felt more scars on his bare back, and also small craters where blisters had been raised by the mustard gas.

He said: We are supposed to go on parade, marching in lockstep, one battalion after another, as if war is an orderly thing, as if there has been a victory. I will not parade. It is for idiots.

But we won, I said. It's Armistice.

You want my rifle? Here. And he thrust it into my hands.

This heavy rifle actually fired in the Great War. He was supposed to have stowed it at the armory on Sixty-seventh Street. Then I felt his overseas cap fitted on my head. Then suddenly his tunic was hanging off my shoulder. I felt ashamed that for all the accounts of the newspapers' war that Julia read to me in her Hungarian accent at the breakfast table each morning, I had still not understood what it was like over there. Langley would tell me through the following weeks, interrupted occasionally by poundings on the door by the army constabulary for he had left his unit before being legally mustered out and given his discharge papers, and of all the difficulties with the law we were to endure in the years to come, this one, the matter of his technical desertion, was like the preview.

Each time I answered and swore that I hadn't seen my brother, and that was no lie. And they would notice me looking at the sky as I spoke and would beat a retreat.

And when the Armistice Day parade was held, and I could hear the excitement in the city, people hurrying past our house, the cars crawling, their horns blowing, and through all of that the distant strains of military march music, I heard from Langley, as if antiphonically, of his experiences. I would not have asked him about it, I wanted him to be his old self, I recognized that he needed to recover. He had not known till he came back that our parents had succumbed to the flu. So that was another something he had to deal with. He slept a lot and didn't take any notice of Julia, at least at first, although he might have found it odd to see her serving dinner and then sitting down to join us. So with all of that, without any prompting, while the city turned out for the victory parade, he told me about the war in his hoarse voice, which would at times drift into a whisper or a wheeze before recovering its gravelly tone. At moments it was more as if he was talking to himself.

He said they couldn't keep their feet dry. It was too cold to take off your shoes, there was ice in the trench, ice water and ice. You got trench foot. Your feet swelled and turned blue.

There were rats. Big brown ones. They ate the dead, they were fearless. Bite through the canvas sacks to get at the human meat. Once, with an officer in his wood coffin and the lid not fast, they nosed it back and in a minute the coffin was filled with a hump of squealing rats squirming and wiggling and fighting, a wormy mass of brown and black rat slime turning red with blood. The officers shot into the mass with their pistols with the rats pouring over the sides and then someone leapt forward and slammed the coffin lid back down and they nailed it shut with the officer and the dead and dying rats together.

Attacks always came before dawn. First there would be heavy bombardment, field guns, mortars, and then the lines advancing out of the smoke and mist to go down under the machine-gun fire. Langley learning to lean back against the front wall of the trench so as to catch the Kraut with his bayonet as the man leapt over him, like the bull goring the bullfighter in the buttocks or in the thigh, or worse, and even losing hold of the rifle when the poor fool took the bayonet with him as he fell.

Langley was almost court-martialed for seeming to threaten an officer. He had said, Why am I killing men I don't know? You have to know someone to want to kill him. For this aperçu he was sent out on patrol night after night, crawling over a furrowed blasted plain of mud and barbed wire, pressing himself to the ground when the Very flares lit up the sky.

And then that one morning of the yellow fog that didn't seem to be much of anything. It hardly smelled at all. It dissipated soon enough and then your skin began to burn.

And to what purpose, Langley said to himself. You watch, you'll see.

As I have, simply by living on.

On the day Langley went by himself up to the Woodlawn Cemetery to visit our parents' graves, I placed his Springfield rifle on the fireplace mantel in the drawing room and there it has stayed, almost the first piece in the collection of artifacts from our American life.

THE FACT THAT I had taken up with Julia had not sat well with the senior maid, Siobhan, who was used to giving the orders in their household world of designated responsibilities. Julia, risen from my bed, had assumed an elevated status for herself and was disinclined to be ordered about. Her attitude amounted to insurgency. Siobhan had been in our employ far longer and as she told me tearfully one day, my mother had not only found her work exceptional but had come to feel about her that she was like a member of the family. I had known nothing of this. I knew Siobhan only by her voice, which, without thinking much about it, I had found unattractive, a thin high whiny voice, and I knew she was a stout woman by the way she breathed from the slightest exertion. Also there was a smell about her, not that she was unclean but that her pores produced a kind of steambath redolence that remained in a room after she had left it. However, with Langley's return I was intent on keeping peace in our house, for his gloomy presence and irritability with every little thing had unbalanced us all, including, I might say, the Negro cook, Mrs. Robileaux, who prepared what she wanted to prepare and served what she wanted to serve without advice from anyone, including Langley, who kept pushing his plate aside and leaving the table. So there were undercurrents of dissatisfaction coming from all directions—we were a household already far removed from that of my parents, of whose orderly administration and regally stolid ways I found myself newly appreciative. But not having the faintest idea of how to deal with any of this emotional disorder, I made a mental distinction between anarchy and evolutionary change. The one was the world falling to pieces, the other was only the inevitable creep of time, which was what we had now in this house, I decided, the turning over of the seconds and minutes of life to show its ever new guise. This was my rationalization for doing nothing. Langley was privileged by his veterancy and Mrs. Robileaux by her cooking skills. I should have done something to support Siobhan but instead found my own guilty solace in looking away and accepting Julia on her own terms.

The girl was amatory in a matter-of-fact way. I had heard about Europeans that they didn't make as much of a fuss about lovemaking as our women did, they just went ahead and accepted it as another appetite, as natural as hunger or thirst. So call Julia naughty by nature, but more than that, ambitious, which is why, having achieved my bed, she began to lord it over Siobhan as if in practice for the position of lady of the house. I knew that of course, I am only blind of eye. But I admired the immigrant verve of her. She had come to America under the auspices of a servant supply agency and had made a life for herself working first for a family my family knew, and then after they had moved themselves to Paris, arriving at our door with excellent references. I am sure Julia was older than I by some five or six years. However languorously attentive she was at night, she was up promptly at dawn and returned to her household responsibilities. I would lie there in the still warm sheets where she had lain and compose her image from the lingering tangy smell of her and from what my hands had learned of her person. She had tiny ears and a plump mouth. When we lay head to head, her toes barely reached my ankle bones. But she was generously proportioned, the flesh of her shoulders and arms giving under the lightest pressure of my thumbs. She was short-waisted, high-breasted, and with a firm backside and sturdy thighs and calves. She did not have an elegant foot, it was rather wide and, unlike the smooth soft rest of her, somewhat rough to the touch. Her straight hair when unbound fell below her shoulders—she would arrange herself on all fours above my recumbent form and flip her hair over her face so as to brush my chest and belly, sweeping her hair one way and then the other with a shake of her head. At such times she would murmur sentences which began in English and drifted into Hungarian. Like you this, sir, does the sir like his Julia? And somewhere along the line without my realizing it she would have reverted to her Hungarian, whispering her quizzical endearments as to whether I liked what she was doing so that I imagined I was literate in the Hungarian language. I would pull her down so as to get the same brushing effect from her nipples while her hair lay about my face and in my mouth. We did lots of creative things and kept each other amused well enough. The inside of her fit me rather well. She told me her hair was very light, the color of wheat—she said *veet*—and that her eyes were gray like a cat.

It was Julia's warm and compliant body and immigrant murmurings that persuaded me to put out of mind the slow grinding away of Siobhan's honor as her and Julia's places in the household scheme of things were reversed and Siobhan was the one who found herself taking orders. This good woman had only two recourses, to quit our employ or to pray. But she was a single Irishwoman of middle or even late middle age, with no family as far as I knew. The years of employment in this house had been her life. In such circumstances people cling however unhappily to their jobs and save their money, coin by coin, against the time when they hope to have a decent burial. I did remember that when my mother died, it was Siobhan who wept piteously at the grave, she, Siobhan, as sentimental about death as only the deeply religious can be. And so, finally, prayer would be the means by which she would endure the profound offense to her pride of place and sense of possession of the house that a good servant has who is responsible for its upkeep. And if her prayers looked toward her restoration or, at moments of bitterness that would later have to be confessed to the Father, to vengeance, whatever the Lord might saith, I would have to say that they were answered in the Protestant form of Perdita Spence, a friend of Langley's from childhood whom he had escorted at her coming out, and who now appeared for dinner one night at his invitation.

For as the weeks had passed Langley had begun to emerge from his doldrums. Not that you would hear him whistling or finding a reason to be excited about something, but his acerb intelligence was honing up as in the old days. Perdita Spence had stood in his consideration ever since their teens and that I suppose was the closest he could come to an outright feeling for her. I had seen her in our home once or twice before my eyes darkened and I projected that memory now, adding mentally to her age by listening to her conversation. I remembered her main features, which were a long nose and eyes set too close together and shoulders that looked as if she wore epaulets under her shirtwaist. I seem also to have an image in my mind of Miss Spence marching arm in arm with the suffragettes down Fifth Avenue, but that may be an embellishment of my own making. I do know that she was a comfortable height for Langley, who was a six-footer. So she was tall for a woman and, as I listened to her remarks before dinner about the society of which our two families had been a part, I thought that she was the perfect social match as well—someone who in her person invoked the life Langley had lived before he went to war, and so just what he needed to palliate the dark instincts of his own mind.

Langley and I had both dressed for dinner and I had somehow imposed upon Julia and Siobhan an armistice of their own so that they could together spruce up the place, which they did apparently, for I smelled the furniture polish on my Aeolian, and the hearth fires in the study and living room were without the choking fumes I had come to expect. Langley had said enough to Mrs. Robileaux to have her fulfill his menu, which consisted of oysters on the half shell, a sorrel soup, and a roast with potato soufflé and peas in the pod. And he had gone to the cellar for a white and a red. But all of Perdita Spence's chatter ceased abruptly when Julia, after serving the first two courses, brought out the roast and joined us at the table. I heard the scraping of Julia's chair, a delicate cough, and even, perhaps, her deferential smile.

After a long silence Perdita Spence said: How novel, Langley, to put your guests to work. But where is my apron?

Langley: Julia is not a guest.

Miss Perdita Spence: Oh?

Langley: When serving she is one of the staff. When seated she is Homer's inamorata.

It's a kind of hybrid situation, I said by way of clarifying things.

There was silence. I heard not even a wine sip.

And after all, said Langley, human identity is a mysterious thing. Can we even be sure there is something called the Self?

Miss Perdita Spence's peroration, addressed only to Langley, the one person in the room high enough in her estimation to have her opinion, was actually quite interesting. There was not the umbrage you would expect from someone of her class finding herself at table with a servant. She said—and I can only paraphrase after these many years—that given brother Homer's deficient state she could understand his availing himself of whatever poor creature came to hand. But to sit this same creature at the dinner table was the boorish act of a pasha for whom it was not enough to exercise his power, he must also put it on display. Here was this immigrant woman, who had to bend to his will lest she lose her job, sat down to her obvious discomfort in order to advertise her total servitude. A woman is not a pet monkey, said Miss Spence, and if she is to be used to her shame at least let it be in the dark, where no one can hear her weeping but her abuser.

I'll take you home, said Langley.

And so the dinner was left to my inamorata and me. Julia filled my plate and sat herself beside me. Not a word was spoken, we knew what we had to do. With Mrs. Robileaux coming out of the kitchen periodically to stand at the doorway and glare at us, we proceeded to eat for four.

I had no idea what Julia was thinking. Surely she had gotten the gist of Miss Spence's critique, but I sensed her indifference as if she, Julia, couldn't have cared less what this stranger had to say. She went about dinner with the same gusto with which she cleaned house or made love, refilling my wine glass, and then her own, serving me another cut of the roast before replenishing her own plate.

And now here is the sequence of thoughts I had, for I remember them quite clearly. I recalled that Julia had appeared unsummoned in my bedroom the evening of the day I had asked to touch her face. I had not meant anything by that, I merely wanted information, I like to know what the people around me look like. I had felt her jaw, which was large, and her wide full mouth and her small ears and slightly splayed nose and her forehead which was broad, with a high hairline. And that same night she had slipped into my bed and waited.

Was Perdita Spence right—that this immigrant girl in order to keep her job was merely responding to what she thought was a summons? Langley hadn't believed that—he had seen the assertiveness of the maid, who in a relatively short time had taken charge of the household and bedded his brother.

But now here is what happened: In the process of leaving a clean plate, I was working on the last of the pea pods, crunching them in my teeth and savoring their sweet green bitter-edged juices, and all at once I found myself thinking of the truck farm at the corner of Madison Avenue and Ninety-fourth Street, where as a sighted child I would go along the rows with my mother in the early autumn to pick the vegetables for our table. I'd pull the carrot bunches out of the soft ground, pluck the tomatoes from their vines, uncover the yellow summer squash hiding beneath their leaves, scoop up the heads of lettuce with both hands. And we so enjoyed ourselves at these times, my mother and I, as she held her basket out for me to deposit what I had chosen. Some of the plants rose above my head and the sun-warmed leaves would brush my cheeks. I chewed the tiny leaves of herbs, I was made giddy by the profusion of vivid colors and the humid smell of leaf and root and moist soil on a sunny day. Of course, along with my sight, that farm had long since gone, an armory in its place, and I suppose it was the

wine that was allowing me to dredge from the depths of my un-
forgiving mind the image of my gracious mother when she was
in such uncharacteristically loving companionship with her
small son.

Taking hold of Julia's capable hand in this emotional moment of recall, I found my palm resting not on flesh but on
stone. It was a ring the maid wore and, as I circled it with three
fingers the better to understand its size and shape, I realized it
was the heavy diamond ring of my mother's that had shot
shards of sunlight into my eyes as she held the handle of our
garden basket.

Julia murmured, Ah dear surr or something of the sort and I
felt her other hand on my cheek as she gently tried to disengage
and I just as gently wouldn't let her.

And so this was the extraordinary sequence of events for
which I suppose I have Miss Perdita Spence to thank, although
she is at this date no longer among the living. Or perhaps it was
my brother's decision to invite her for dinner, or perhaps I
should go further back to the war that had so changed him so
that in his gruff uncompromising way he would only half admit
to himself that he might mend, if mend he would, by marrying,
and so begin his grudging quest by renewing his acquaintance
with that tall sharp-shouldered schoolmate of his who did not
condone the depraved doings in our household.

We had a trial, naturally, Langley and I the sitting judges,
Siobhan the prosecuting attorney. This was in the library, where
the shelved books, the globe, the portraits served for a juridical
setting. Julia, my Hungarian darling, wept as she claimed it was

Siobhan's idea to lend her the ring from my mother's jewelry case so she, Julia, could be more the table guest than the serving maid. It would be a kind of credential, she insisted, although that word was not in her vocabulary. To look so Mr. Homer surr and I was to be marry, is what she actually said. I might have decided to take her side, but my own credibility as a responsible member of this household had been seriously damaged when I'd had to admit to Langley that I had forgotten about my mother's jewelry when I'd settled her estate, and so it had remained, subject to theft, in the small unlocked wall safe in her bedroom behind a portrait of a great-aunt of hers who had achieved some notoriety by riding camelback across the Sudan for what reason nobody quite knew.

Siobhan denied having bestowed the ring on the girl, who, she said, had access to the entire house as the self-appointed maid in authority and could have noseyed about my mother's bedroom without anyone being any the wiser. Siobhan reminded everyone how long she had been in service to this family as opposed to this thief who was trying to make her out as some devilish conspirator. And why would I myself help this slattern, she being the thief she is, said Siobhan.

Langley, he of the judicious temperament, said to Siobhan, Petitio principii—you assume in your premise what you have to establish in your conclusion.

That may be, Mr. Collyer, said she, but I know what I know. And so the case was made.

Langley afterward took the jewel case, which contained not just that ring, but brooches, bracelets, pairs of earrings, and a diamond tiara, and put it in a safe deposit box at the Corn Exchange against the time when we might need to sell these things—a time I couldn't imagine ever coming, and which of course did come and fairly promptly at that.

And now my sweet weeping hard-nippled and felonious bed mate was gone from the premises as unceremoniously as Miss Perdita Spence, as if they were prototypes of the gender with which, through the years, Langley and I would, on one basis or another, find ourselves incompatible.

ONLY AFTER JULIA HAD packed and left did I feel really stupid. As if her absence brought her into moral clarity. While consorting with her I'd had no idea of who she was—she was a presence fragmented by my self-satisfaction—but now, as I reflected on her frustrated ambition, the almond smell of her and the places on her body that I'd held in my hands coalesced into a person by whom I felt betrayed. This immigrant woman with her strategies. She had set forth on this domestic field of battle with a battle plan. Rather than maid-servant who in fear of being thrown out in the street gives in to her master's desires, she was in service only to herself, an actress, a performer, playing a role.

I asked Langley to describe her appearance. A sturdy little thing, he said. Brown hair much too long, she had to wind it around and pin it up under that cap and of course it didn't quite work and so with strands and curls hanging about her face and neck she drew attention to herself as a servant never would who knows her place. We should have had her cut her hair.

But then she wouldn't have been Julia, I said. And she told me her hair was the color of wheat.

A dull dark brown, Langley said.

And her eyes?

I didn't notice the color of her eyes. Except that they glanced around constantly as if she was talking to herself in the Hungarian language. We had to fire her, Homer, she was too smart to trust. But I'll give you this: it is the immigrant hordes who keep this country alive, the waves of them arriving year after year. We had to fire the girl, but in fact she demonstrates the genius of our national immigration policy. Who believes in America more than the people who run down the gangplank and kiss the ground?

She didn't even say goodbye.

Well there you have it. She'll be rich someday.

FOR CONSOLATION I DOVE into my music, but for the first time in my life it failed me. I decided the Aeolian needed tuning. We summoned Pascal, the piano tuner, a prissy little Belgian drenched in a cologne that lingered in the music room for days afterward. *Il n'y a rien mal avec ce piano,* he said, as I assemble him in my bad French. By calling him to review his unerring work I had insulted him. In fact the problem was not the piano, it was my repertoire, which consisted entirely of works I had learned when I could still read music. It was no longer enough for me. I was restless. I needed to work on new pieces.

A society for the blind had gotten a music publisher to print works in musical Braille. So I ordered some music. But it was no use—though I could read Braille, my fingers wouldn't translate the little dots into sounds. The notations would not combine, each somehow stood alone, and anything contrapuntal was beyond me.

Here is where Langley came to the rescue. He found at some estate auction a player piano, an upright. It came with dozens of perforated paper scrolls on cylinders. You fitted the cylinders on two dowels, the scroll running athwart, you pumped the foot pedals, the keys depressed as if by magic, and what you heard was a performance of one of the greats, Paderewski, Anton Rubinstein, Josef Hoffmann, as if they were sitting right there beside you on the piano bench. In this way I added to my repertoire, listening to the piano rolls over and over until I could place my fingers on the keys precisely at the moment they were mechanically pressed. Then finally, I could turn to my own Aeolian and play the piece for myself, in my own interpretation. I mastered any number of Schubert impromptus, Chopin études, Mozart sonatas, and I and my music were in accord once again.

The player piano was the first of many pianos Langley was to collect over the years—there are a good dozen here, in whole or in part. He may have had my interests in mind when he began, possibly he believed that there had to be somewhere in the world a better-sounding piano than my Aeolian. Of course there wasn't though I dutifully tried each one he brought home.

If I didn't like it he stripped it down to its innards to see what could be done and so came to see pianos as machines, music-making machines, to be taken apart and wondered at and put back together. Or not. When Langley brings something into the house that has caught his fancy—a piano, a toaster, a Chinese bronze horse, a set of encyclopedias—that is just the beginning. Whatever it is, it will be acquired in several versions because until he loses his interest and goes on to something else he'll be looking for its ultimate expression. I think there may be a genetic basis for this. Our father collected things as well, for along with the many shelves of medical volumes in his study are stoppered glass jars of fetuses, brains, gonads, and various other organs preserved in formaldehyde—all apropos of his professional interests, of course. Still, I can't really believe that Langley doesn't bring to his passion for collecting things something entirely his own: he is morbidly thrifty—ever since we've been running this household ourselves he's worried about our finances. Saving money, saving things, finding value in things other people have thrown away or that may be of future use in one way or another—that's part of it too. As you might expect of an archivist of the daily papers, Langley has a world view and since I don't have one of my own I have always gone along with what he does. I knew someday it would all become as logical and sound and sensible to me as it was to him. And that has long since come to pass. Jacqueline, my muse, I speak to you directly for a moment: You have looked in on this house. You know there is just no other way for us to be. You know it is who we are. Langley is my older brother. He is a veteran who served bravely in the Great War and lost his health for his efforts. When we were young what he collected, what he brought home, were those thin volumes of verse that he read to his blind brother. Here's a line: "Doom is dark and deeper than any sea-dingle . . ."

MY EXPANDED REPERTOIRE came in very handy when I took a job playing piano for silent movies, where I had to improvise pieces according to the nature of the scene being shown. If it was a love scene I would play, say, Schumann's "Träumerei," if it was a fight scene, the fast movement of a furious late Beethoven, if soldiers were marching, I'd march with them, and if there was a glorious finale I could improvise the last movement of Beethoven's Ninth.

You will ask how I could know what was up on the screen. It was a girl we had hired, a music student who sat beside me and told me sotto voce exactly what was going on. Now a funny chase with people falling out of cars, she would say, or here comes the hero riding a horse at a gallop, or the firemen are sliding down a pole, or—and here she would lower her voice and touch my shoulder—the lovers are embracing and looking into each other's eyes and the card says "I love you."

Langley had found this student in the Hoffner-Rosenblatt Music School on West Fifty-ninth Street, and because in this time I am describing, the diminishing legacy of our parents due to some unfortunate investments had become apparent to us— which is why I had taken the job at this movie theater on Third Avenue, playing three complete shows from late afternoon into the evening, every weekend from Friday to Sunday—we did not pay her, my movie eyes, this girl Mary, only in coinage, we supplemented her small salary with free lessons given by me in our home. Since she lived with her grandmother and younger brother across town, on the far West Side, in Hell's Kitchen in fact, in what had to be modest circumstances, her grandmother was only too happy not to have to pay for Mary's lessons any

rant family that had suffered major
arents having died, her father from
where he worked, and his widow
ncer not long after that. And of
her the streetcar fare, and because
to the girl, almost as if she were a
with us. Her name was Mary Eliz-
teen at the time, a parochial school
unts the prettiest thing, with black
in and pale blue eyes and her head
roud posture, as if her slight frame
server that here was a weakness that
f. But when we walked together to

and from the movie theater, she held my arm as if we were a couple, and of course I fell in love with her, though not daring to do anything about it, being in my late twenties by now and beginning to lose my hair.

I wouldn't say Mary Riordan was an outstanding student of the piano, though she loved playing. In fact she was more than competent. I just felt her attack was not assertive enough, though when she worked on something like Debussy's Sunken

Cathedral, her sensitive touch seemed justified. She was just a gentle soul in all her ways. Her goodness was like the fragrance of pure unscented soap. And she understood as I did that when you sat down and put your hands on the keys, it was not just a piano in front of you, it was a universe.

How easily and with such grace she accommodated herself to her situation. After all, what an odd household we were, with these many rooms that must have seemed daunting to a child from the tenements, and a serving woman who had instantly adopted her and given her chores as a mother would do, and a cook whose characteristic glower did not change from morning till night. And a blind man whom she led to and from his job, and an iconoclast with a loud cough and a hoarse voice who rushed out every day, morning and evening, to buy every newspaper published in the city.

Often when I sat next to her for her lesson I would fall into a reverie and just let her play without any instruction at all. Langley fell in love with her too—I could tell by his tendency to lecture when she was present. Langley's improvised theories of music did not persuade the two of us, who could transmogrify instantly into the sinuous skein of "Jesu, Joy of Man's Desiring." He would insist, for example, that when prehistoric man discovered that he could make sounds by singing or beating on something or blowing through the end of a fossilized leg bone, his intention was to sound the vast emptiness of this strange world by saying "I am here, I am here!" Even your Bach, even your precious Mozart in his waistcoat and knee britches and silk stockings was doing no more than that, Langley said.

We listened patiently to my brother's ideas but said nothing and, when nothing further was said, went back to our lesson. On one occasion Mary couldn't quite suppress a sigh, which sent Langley mumbling back to his newspapers. He and I were competing for the girl, of course, but it was a competition neither of us could win. We knew that. We didn't talk about it but we both knew we suffered a passion that would destroy this girl if we ever acted upon it. I had come dangerously close. The little movie theater was right under the Third Avenue El. Every few minutes a train would roar overhead and on one occasion I pretended I couldn't hear what Mary was saying. Still playing with my left hand, I took my right hand off the keys and pressed her frail shoulder till her face was close to mine and her lips brushed my ear. It was all I could do not to take her in my arms. I was almost made ill by my heedlessness. I atoned by buying her an ice cream on the way home. She was a brave but wounded thing, legally an orphan. We were in loco parentis, and always would be. She had her own room up on the top floor next to Siobhan's and I would think of her sleeping there, chaste and beautiful, and wonder if the Catholics were not right in deifying virginity and if Mary's parents had not been wise in conferring upon her frail beauty the protective name of the mother of their God.

HOW LONG MARY ELIZABETH lived with us I don't quite remember but when I was fired from my job at the little movie theater on Third Avenue—the talkies had come along, you see—Langley and I sat down and agreed there was no call to keep her with us anymore—really it was more for our sake that we came to this decision—and allotting the necessary sums from our diminishing resources, we sent her off to the Sisters of Mercy Junior College in Westchester County, where she would study music and French and moral philosophy and whatever other educative things would assure her of a better existence. She was grateful and not too sad, having learned from her grandmother that as an orphan she should expect to be trundled off from one institution to another in hopes someday of finding a permanence that would answer her prayers.

Her gentle touch at the piano was something I should not have questioned. She was feeling her way through music as through life, a parentless child trying to regain a belief in a reasonable world. But she did not make others feel sad for her, nor did she allow herself to be as self-involved as she had every right to be. She was staunchly cheerful. When we had walked together to the theater, she held my arm as if I was escorting her as a man escorts a woman. She matched her gait to mine, as people do when they are couples. She knew I was proud of my ability to get around town and when I made a mistake, intending to cross the street at the wrong time, or stepping on someone's heels—because I tended to walk with the assurance of a sighted person—she would stop me or steer me with the slightest pressure of her hand. And she would say something as if what had just transpired had not happened at all. That Buster, she would say—as if she hadn't heard the horn that had blown or the driver who had cursed—that Buster, he's so funny. He gets into these scrapes and just barely escapes with his life and the expression on his face never changes. And you know he loves the girl and doesn't know what to do about it. That's so sweet and dopey. I'm glad it's still playing. I could watch it forever. And you play just the right accompaniment, Uncle Homer. He should come down from the screen and shake your hand, I mean it.

I CANNOT AT THIS moment bear to speak of what became of Mary Elizabeth Riordan. Not a night passes that I don't recall how, when she was going off to school, we all stood with her on the sidewalk waiting for a taxicab that would take her and her one suitcase to Grand Central Terminal. I heard a cab pull up and everyone saying goodbye, Langley clearing his throat and Siobhan who cried, and Mrs. Robileaux blessing her from the doorway at the top of the steps. They told me how lovely Mary looked in the smart tailored coat that had been our gift. She was hatless on this chilly sunny September morning. You could feel both the warmth and the breeze blowing through it. I touched her hair and felt soft wisps of it lifting. And when I took her face in my hands—the lovely thin face and resolute chin, her temples with their soft and steady pulse, the slim straight nose and her soft smiling lips—she took my hand and kissed it. Goodbye, goodbye, I whisper to myself. Goodbye, my love, my girl, my dear one. Goodbye. As if it is happening at this moment.

BUT MEMORIES ARE not temporally driven, they detach themselves from time, and all of that was much later than our recklessly spendthrift years when Langley and I went out almost every night to one nightclub or another where ladies with rolled stockings and short skirts sat on your lap and blew smoke in your face and surreptitiously felt along the inside of your thigh to see what you had there. Some of the clubs were rather elegant, with a pretty good kitchen and a dance floor, others were basement dives where the music came from a radio on a wall shelf broadcasting some swing orchestra from Pittsburgh. But where you went didn't matter, you could die of the gin in any of these joints, and the mood was the same everywhere, people laughing at what wasn't funny. But it felt good to establish yourself in this or that club, to be let in the door and be greeted like someone important. In these peculiar nights of Prohibition, the law only had to say No Drinking to get everybody plastered. Langley said the speakeasy was the true democratic melting pot. And it was true, at this one club, the Cat's Whiskers, I became friendly with a gangster who said to call him Vincent. I knew he was the real thing because when he laughed other men at the table laughed with him. He was very interested in my sightlessness, this Vincent. What's it like without eyes, he said. I told him it wasn't so bad, that I made up for it other ways. How, he said. I told him that when I had a few drinks I regained something like vision. In fact I believed this. I knew I was hallucinating, I was seeing all right but into my own mind of thought and impression as I generated visions from what I learned from my other senses and added, by way of detail, my judgments of character and my attraction to this one or revulsion for that one. Of course when you're sober you make the same deductions, I know that, but at these times my brain synapses firing with the fumes of alcohol, a clarity of organized impressions amounted to a kind of vision. Naturally I didn't go into all that, I just said that with a lot of noise and music and booze, of course, and cigarette smoke heavy enough to float in, I could make shadows out pretty well.

How many fingers am I holding up, he said. None, I said. I knew that old trick. He chuckled and slapped me on the shoulder. This bozo's smart, he said. He had a thin whispery voice, tuneless except for a whistle that ran along the top of it as if one of his lungs had sprung a leak. He lit a match and held it up to my face to see the clouds in my eyes. He asked me to describe what he looked like. I reached out to touch his face and one of his henchmen yelled and grabbed my wrist. We don't do that, he said. It's okay, letim, Vincent said and so I touched his face, and felt sunken cheeks with pockmarks, a sharp recessive chin, a beaky nose, the head widening at the top and thick wavy wetted hair that rose back from a widow's peak like feathers. He was all hunched over to accommodate me and I thought of a hawk maybe dressed in a suit and a shirt with cuff links. I told him that and he laughed.

It was exciting talking to him like he was a normal person—sitting and chatting with someone you knew had no regard for the life of anyone he might disagree with. I found it to be true generally with the criminals we ran into that as a class they were extremely sensitive. The thought that I might inadvertently offend Vincent was exhilarating and made me careless of what I said. But showing no deference turned out to be the right way to deal with him. And I didn't ask questions, I didn't ask him as you might, with a normal person, what he did, what his profession was. It didn't matter, did it? Whatever it was it made him a gangster. This was the kind of excitement Langley and I looked for when we went out in those days and were still expecting a return from social life. It was like what a lion tamer must feel when the beast is sitting on its stool but at any moment might leap for his throat. Vincent kept plying me with drinks. I was one of his entertainments, a blind man who could see. He was in effect holding court because people came over to say hello. A woman he knew took up residence on his lap, and so he had a new diversion. I could smell them both in all their glory, his cigar, her cigarette, the pomade on his hair, her gin reek. Her abrupt silences in mid-sentence told me he had his hand up her dress. Around me the noise was instructive. This was an elegant club for a speakeasy, it had a lively if predictable dance orchestra, a lot of bounce, the rhythm section predominating, a banjo, a string bass. The music was fast and mechanical though the dancers didn't seem to mind, they hopped and stomped about, their feet thumping the floor on the downbeat. But also glasses were breaking, and the occasional shout and scuffle indicated to me the place might blow at any time. And there was always the possibility of a police raid though probably not with such as Vincent in the room. And then this girl who had settled on his lap, after a while I heard her say, You gotta stop that, honey. Oowheee, she said, or else. Or else what, babe, he said. Or else come to the Ladies' with me, she said.

Yes. I do remember that particular evening. When Langley

and I said good night, my new friend Vincent had his car take us home. It was quite a car too, with a deep growl of a motor and plush seats and a man sitting up front next to the driver in some gangland equivalent of livery.

The car pulled up in front of our door and after we got out it idled there for a long minute before it drove off. Langley said, Well that was a mistake. We stood at the top of the stoop. It must have been three in the morning. I had had a good time. The air was brisk. It was sometime early in the spring. I could smell the budding trees across the street in the park. I breathed in deeply. I felt strong. I was strong, I was young and strong. I asked Langley why it was a mistake. I don't like it that now those scum know where we live, Langley said.

LANGLEY DID NOT SCOFF at my claim to be able to see when I had had a few. You know, Homer, he said, among the philosophers there is endless debate as to whether we see the real world or only the world as it appears in our minds, which is not necessarily the same thing. So if that's the case, if the real world is A, and what we see projected on our minds is B, and that's the best we can hope for, then it's not just your problem.

Well, I said, maybe it'll turn out I have eyes as good as anyone's.

Yes and maybe someday you, as you grow older and know more, have more experiences stored in your brain, you should be able to see in sobriety what now you see when plastered.

Langley was convinced of this because it fit right in with his

Theory of Replacements, which he had by now developed into a metaphysical sort of idea of the repetition or recurrence of life events, the same things happening over and over, especially given the proscribed limits of human intelligence, *Homo sapiens* being a specie that, in his words, just didn't have enough. So that what you knew from the past could be applied to the present. My deductive visions were in accord with Langley's major project, the collection of the daily papers with the ultimate aim of creating one day's edition of a newspaper that could be read forevermore as sufficient to any day thereof.

I will speak for a moment about this because while Langley had many projects, as befitting a mind as restless as his, this one endured. His interest never flagged from the very first day he went out to buy the morning papers to the end of his life when his newspaper bales and boxes of clippings rose from floor to ceiling in every room of our house.

Langley's project consisted of counting and filing news stories according to category: invasions, wars, mass murders, auto, train, and plane wrecks, love scandals, church scandals, robberies, murders, lynchings, rapes, political misdoings with a subhead of crooked elections, police misdeeds, gangland rubouts, investment scams, strikes, tenement fires, trials civil, trials criminal, and so on. There was a separate category for natural disasters such as epidemics, earthquakes, and hurricanes. I can't remember what all the categories were. As he explained, eventually—he did not say when—he would have enough statistical evidence to narrow his findings to the kinds of events that were, by their frequency, seminal human behavior. He would then run further statistical comparisons until his order of templates was fixed so that he would know which stories should go on the front page, which on the second page, and so on. Photographs too had to be annotated and chosen for their typicality, but this, he acknowledged, was difficult. Maybe he wouldn't use photographs. It was a huge enterprise and occupied him for several hours each day. He would run out for all the morning papers, and in the afternoon for the evening papers, and then there were the business papers, the sex gazettes, the freak sheets, the vaudeville papers, and so on. He wanted to fix American life finally in one edition, what he called Collyer's eternally current dateless newspaper, the only newspaper anyone would ever need.

For five cents, Langley said, the reader will have a portrait in newsprint of our life on earth. The stories will not have overly particular details as you find in ordinary daily rags, because the real news here is of the Universal Forms of which any particular detail would only be an example. The reader will always be up to date, and au courant with what is going on. He will be assured that he reads of indisputable truths of the day including that of his own impending death, which will be dutifully recorded as a number in the blank box on the last page under the heading Obituaries.

Of course I was dubious about all of this. Who would want to buy such a newspaper? I couldn't imagine a news story that assured you that something was happening but didn't tell you where or when or to whom it was happening.

My brother laughed. But Homer, he said, wouldn't you spend a nickel for such a paper if you didn't have to buy another ever again? I admit this would be bad for the fish business but we have to think always of the greatest good for the greatest number.

What about sports? I said.

Whatever the sport is, said Langley, someone wins and someone loses.

What about art?

If it is art, it will offend before it is revered. There are calls for its destruction and then the bidding begins.

What if something comes along that has no precedent, I said. Where will your newspaper be then?

Like what?

Like Darwin's Theory of Evolution. Like that Einstein fellow's Theory of Relativity.

Well you could say these theories replace the old ones. Albert Einstein replaces Newton, and Darwin replaces Genesis. Not that anything has been made clearer. But I'll give you that both theories are unprecedented. What of it? What do we really know? If every question is answered so that we know everything there is to know about life and the universe, what then? What will be different? It will be like knowing how a combustion engine works. That's all. The darkness will be there still.

What darkness? I said.

The deepest darkness. You know: the darkness deeper than any sea-dingle.

Langley would never complete his newspaper project. I knew that and I'm sure he knew it as well. It was a crazy foolish hand-rubbing scheme that kept his mind in the mood he liked to be in. It seemed to give him the mental boost he needed to keep going—working on something that had no end other than to systematize his grim view of life. His energies sometimes seemed unnatural to me. As if he did all the things he did to keep himself among the living. Even so he would slip for days at a time into a discouraging lassitude. Discouraging to me, I mean. I would catch it sometimes. Nothing would seem to be worth doing and the house would be like a tomb.

NOR WAS THERE any true consolation to be had in the whores that none other than Vincent, the gangster with the squeaky voice, sent over one night as a present to me, his best blind friend. Jacqueline, you will have to forgive this: but you did tell me to be fearless and write what comes to mind. There they were at the door as our clocks struck midnight, two girls whose broad smiles I could hear, and with a big cake on a rolling table that the same driver who had brought us home a month before rattled into the hall, and a half dozen bottles of champagne packed in ice.

It takes some drinking to dissolve the wariness that comes over one who is the recipient of a gift from a gangster. It wasn't my birthday, first of all, and second of all, because some time had passed since the night we had met Vincent, what other inference was possible than that (a) we were now a pin on his map, and (b) without any choice in the matter we could be incurring some mysterious obligation.

These ladies for their part seemed wary of us, or perhaps of our residence, Fifth Avenue on the outside and something of an aspiring warehouse on the inside. Langley and I sat them down in the music room and excused ourselves for a conference. Fortunately both Siobhan and Mrs. Robileaux were long since retired, so that was not the problem. The problem was that these professionals could not be turned away without offending a man of great and possibly murderous sensitivity. As we discussed this dilemma in the butler's pantry I heard Langley putting champagne glasses on a tray and so it wasn't to be that much of a conference after all.

I will say in our defense that at this time we were still young men, relatively speaking, and deprived for some time of the male's basic means of expression. And if this gesture by a man we hardly knew seemed menacingly excessive, there was such a thing as potlatch among indigenous tribes, a means of self-aggrandizement through the distribution of wealth, and who was this Vincent but a sort of tribal sachem determined to elevate himself in the opinions of others. And so we drank the champagne, which had the effect of erasing all thoughts not of the present moment. For this one night we were to arise from our gloom, recklessly relaxed and taken with the philosophical conviction that licentious life had something to say for it.

And I'll say this about the girl who came to my bed: she did not find it humiliating to be accompaniment to a three-layer cake and a bottle of champagne. And I knew the name she gave me was fictive. So I had some sense, once the giggling was over and the serious engagement began, that some achieved wisdom governed her life and that she lived apart from what she did for a living. She had grace, she was not vulgar. And the other thing was that she was very kind, and that the professional she was tended to disappear in the simple facts of a small female body. When afterward she kissed my eyes I almost wept with gratitude. After she was gone, when they both had gone and I heard their car driving off, I was fairly sure that Vincent, their employer, could not have known these whores as Langley and I did. It was as if they waxed or waned in their being according to who it was, of what quality of mind, who touched them.

Langley said only about his encounter that it was finally meaningless, two strangers copulating, and one of them for money. He was not prepared to acknowledge our champagne-induced excitements. He was convinced that one way or another we would end up paying for my gangster friend's generosity, and that we had not heard the last of him. I agreed, though with every passing year and no further word from Vincent the Gangster we would quite forget him. But at this time Langley's presentiment seemed all too valid. So that by noon of the next day the tender emotions of my drunken self were unseated and my gloomy spirit had returned to its throne.

IN THESE MANY years since the war Langley had still not found a companion in love. I knew he was looking. For a while he was very serious about a woman named Anna. If she had a last name I would not hear it. When I asked him what she looked like he said, A radical. I first knew of her existence when he began bringing home nothing from his nighttime explorations but handfuls of pamphlets, which he slapped down on the side table just inside the front door. I measured the seriousness of his passion by the uncharacteristic grooming ritual that he performed before going out in the evening. He would call to Siobhan when he couldn't find a tie or wanted a washed shirt.

But he never got anywhere with this courtship. He returned home one evening rather early and came into the music room, where I had been practicing, and sat himself down to listen. So of course I stopped, turned on the bench, and asked him how the evening had gone. She has no time for dinner or anything else, he said. She will see me if I come to a meeting with her. If I stand on a corner with her and give out flyers to passersby. Like I have to pass these tests. I asked her to marry me. You know what her response was? A lecture about how marriage is a legalized form of prostitution. Can you imagine? Are all radicals that insane?

I asked Langley what sort of radical she was. Who knows, he said. What difference does it make? She's some kind of Socialist-anarchist-anarcho-syndicalist-Communist. Unless you're one of them you can't tell exactly what any of them are. When they're not throwing bombs they're busy splitting into factions.

Not long after this Langley asked me one evening if I'd like to go with him over to a pier on Twentieth Street to see Anna off to Russia. She was being deported and he wanted to say goodbye. Let's go, I said. I was curious to meet this woman who had so interested my brother.

We hailed a taxi. I couldn't help thinking of the time we children saw our parents off to England on the *Mauretania*. I'd stopped crying when I saw the massive white hull and four towering red-and-black smokestacks. There were flags everywhere and hundreds of people at the rail waving as this huge ship began with some seemingly great and noble intelligence of its own to slip away from the dock. When her basso horns blew I nearly jumped out of my skin. How wonderful it all was. And nothing like the scene as we arrived at the Twentieth Street pier to say goodbye to Langley's friend Anna. It was raining. There was some sort of demonstration going on. We were pushed back by a police line. We couldn't get close. What a sad-looking tub, Langley said. Her passengers were deportees, a whole boatload of them. They stood at the rail shouting and singing "The Internationale," their socialist anthem. People on the pier sang along, though unsynchronized. It was like hearing the music and then its echo. I don't see her, Langley said. Whistles blew. I heard women crying, I heard cops cursing and using their clubs. In the distance a police siren. It was sickening to sense from the tremors in the air the application of official brute behavior. And then I heard thunder and the rain turned into a downpour. It seemed to me it was the river water swirled into the sky to drop down on us, so rank was the smell.

Langley and I went home and he poured us shots of scotch whiskey. You see, Homer, he said, there's no such thing as an armistice.

THEN CAME A PERIOD when my brother would bring home a woman from one of our nightclub sprees and after enduring her for a week or a month, he would kick her out. He would even marry a lady named Lila van Dijk, who would live with us for a year before he kicked her out.

Almost from the beginning he and Lila van Dijk did not get along. It was not just that she couldn't bear the stacks of newspapers—most women would feel that way who like their ducks in a row. Lila van Dijk had a mind to change everything. She would rearrange the furniture and he would put it all back the way it was. She complained about his coughing. She complained that cigarette ash was everywhere. She complained about Siobhan's cleaning, she complained about Mrs. Robileaux's cooking. She even complained about me: He's just as bad as you are, I heard her say to Langley. She was an imperious little woman who had one leg shorter than the other and so wore a built-up shoe that I would hear tapping up and down the stairs and from one room to another as she went on her tours of inspection. I had intuited nothing about Langley's Anna—an indistinct voice in a shipboard chorus. I knew more than I wanted to know about his Lila van Dijk.

They had married at her parents' estate in Oyster Bay, and though I dressed for the occasion in my summer ducks and blue blazer, Langley stood before the pastor in his usual baggy corduroys and an open shirt with the sleeves rolled. I had tried to dissuade him but to no avail. And though the van Dijks handled it with dignity, pretending to believe their about-to-be son-in-law was dressed in some sort of bohemian Arts and Crafts style, I could tell they were furious.

Lila van Dijk and Langley practiced their debating skills on a daily basis. I'd go to the piano to drown them out, and if that didn't work I'd go for a walk. What brought on the final break between them was our cook Mrs. Robileaux's grandson, Harold, who had arrived from New Orleans with one suitcase and a cornet. Harold Robileaux. Once we realized he was in the house we converted a basement storage room into a place for him to stay. He was a serious musician and he practiced for hours at a time. He was good too. He would take a hymn like "He walks with me / And He talks with me / And He tells me I am His own . . ." slowing the tempo to bring out the pure tones of his cornet, a mellower sound than you'd ever expect from something made of brass. I could tell he really understood and loved this instrument. The music rose up through the walls and spread through the floors so that it seemed as if our house was the instrument. And then after he had gone through a verse or two, which was enough to make you repent of your pagan life, he'd up the tempo with little stuttering syncopations—as in He waw-walks with me, and taw-talks with me and tells me, yes he tells me I'm his own de own doe-in—and from one moment to the next it became a fervently joyous hymn that made you feel like dancing.

I had heard swing on the radio and of course frequented the clubs where there was a dance orchestra, but Harold Robileaux's hymnal improvisations in our basement were my introduction to Negro jazz. I would never master that music myself, the stride piano, the blues, and that later development, boogie-woogie. Eventually Harold, who was very shy, was persuaded to come upstairs to the music room. We tried to play something together but it didn't quite work, I was too thick, I didn't have the ear for what he could do, I could not compose as he could, taking a tune and playing endless variations of it. He would try to get me to join in on this or that piece, he was a gentle fellow of endless patience, but I didn't have it in me, that improvisatory gift, that spirit.

But we got along, Harold and I. He was short, portly of figure, and with a round smooth face with that brown coloration that feels different from white skin, and plump cheeks and thick lips—a perfect physiognomy, breath and embouchure, for his instrument. He would listen to my Bach and say, Uh-huh, tha's right. He was soft-spoken except when he played, and he was young enough to believe that the world would be fair to him if he worked hard and did his best and played his heart out. That's how young he was, though he said he was twenty-three. And his grandmother, why, the minute he was set up in the house her whole personality changed, she adored him and looked on the rest of us with a new forbearance and understanding. We had accepted him without a moment's hesitation even though, as was her wont, she had brought him in and tucked him away for a few days without bothering to inform us. The first we knew of our boarder was when we heard his cornet, and that's when she was reminded to come to us and tell us Harold Robileaux would be staying for a while.

I liked to listen to him play, as Langley did—this was a new feature of our lives. Harold went out every evening to Harlem and eventually he got together with some other young musicians and they formed their own band and came to our house to rehearse. We were all very happy about this except for Lila van Dijk, who couldn't believe that Langley would actually permit the Harold Robileaux Five to come play their vulgar music in the house without consulting her. Then one day Langley opened the front door and let passersby come up who had stopped at the foot of the front stoop to listen, and despite the music and the crowd gathered in the drawing room and the music room—for Langley had opened the sliding doors between them—right in the middle of all that, with the cornet leading and the snare drum and tuba keeping the beat, and my commandeered piano and the soprano saxophone riffling along, and people snapping their fingers in time, I heard with my acute hearing the screeches upstairs of Lila van Dijk and the growly cursing responses of my brother, as they formally went about ending their marriage.

This will cost us a pretty penny, Langley said after Lila was gone. If she'd cried just once, if she had showed any vulnerability whatsoever, I would have tried to see things from her point of view if only out of respect for her womanhood. But she was intractable. Stubborn. Willful.

Homer, maybe can you tell me why I am fatally attracted to women who are no more than mirrors of myself.

THAT DAY WHEN PEOPLE came in from the street to hear the music of the Harold Robileaux Five may have been in the back of Langley's mind when, some years later, he came up with the idea of a weekly tea dance. Or maybe he remembered how

Harold spoke of playing at rent parties in people's apartments in Harlem.

In the old days our parents would throw an occasional tea dance, opening up the public rooms and inviting all their friends over in the late afternoon. My mother used to dress us up for those occasions. She would duly present us to be insincerely complimented by the guests before the governess took us back upstairs. And Langley may have remembered the elegance of those dances and seen something of a business opportunity in reviving the custom. For of course we had done our research, going over to Broadway where a good dozen or so dance halls had sprung up that charged a dime a dance and had women employed there to accommodate the men who came in without a partner of their own. We would each buy a strip of tickets and dance our way through them, surrendering a ticket to each woman we took into our arms for a dance. It was an indifferent experience to say the least, in these drafty second-floor lofts, atmospheric with cigar smoke and odorous bodies, where the music was broadcast over loudspeakers and whoever was playing the records would sometimes forget when a song was over and you heard the click click of the needle on the blank groove or even the loud scrunch as the needle jumped out of the groove and slid across the label at the center of the record. And everyone would stand around and wait for the next record, and after a minute if nothing happened the men would whistle or shout and everyone would start clapping. One of these places had been a skating rink, that's how cavernous and gloomy it was. Langley said it was lit with colored lights that only cheapened everything and that bouncers stood about with their arms folded. The women in these places tended to be bored, I thought, though some worked up enough energy to ask you your name and make small talk. If they were satisfied you weren't a cop they might quietly make you a business proposition, which tended to happen to me more than to Langley since you don't usually find police who are blind. But mostly they were overtired girls who'd clerked in the department stores, or waited tables, or worked in offices as typists, but were now on their uppers and trying to make a little money as piecework dancing partners. They turned in their collected tickets at the end of a shift and got paid accordingly. I could intuit their characters from their physicality, whether they were light to hold and to do the fox-trot with, or tended to lead you rather than be led, or were listless and maybe on some kind of drug, or were heavy and even fat so that you heard their stockings rub on the insides of their thighs as they stepped along with you. And just their hand in your hand told you a lot.

And as you'd suspect, Langley's business idea was to give our dances for people who wouldn't be caught dead in one of those dance halls.

For the first few Tuesday afternoon tea dances, we invited people we knew, like friends of our mother and father's, and whatever members of our own generation they brought with them. Langley and Siobhan converted the dining room, dismantling the dining table that seated eighteen, lining the chairs against the wall, and rolling up the rug. Our parents had hired musicians for their dances—a trio usually of piano, bass, and snare drum, the drummer using the soft whispery brushes—but we had recorded music, because long before this time of the Great Depression, with so many people out of work, and men in suits and ties standing on line at the soup kitchens, Langley had been collecting phonographs, both the old table models that used steel needles and a voice box at the end of a hollow curved chrome arm, and the more up-to-date electric Victrolas, some of them standing on the floor like pieces of furniture, with speakers hidden behind ribbed panels with cloth webbing.

These first dances were strictly social invitations with no charge. During the breaks people sat in the chairs against the wall and sipped their tea and took cookies from the plate Mrs. Robileaux held in front of them. But of course the word spread and after a couple of weeks people were showing up who had no invitation and we began charging admission at the door. It had worked out just as we'd hoped it would.

I should say here that we were distinguished, we two brothers I mean, in having lost a good deal of our money well before the market crash, either from bad investments or our excessive nightclubbing and other spendthrift habits, though in fact we were far from destitute and things were never as bad for us as for other people. Yet Langley was of a mind to worry about finances even if there was nothing seriously to worry about. I was more relaxed and realistic about our situation but I did not argue when he predicted dire poverty for us as he did when going over the bills each month. It was as if he wanted to be as badly off in the Depression as everyone else. He said, You see,

Homer, how in those dance halls they make money from people who don't have any? We can do that too!

Eventually things were going so well that there were too many dancers for the dining room, and so the drawing room and parlor were similarly stripped. Poor Siobhan was at the end of her endurance, shoving furniture into corners and rolling rugs and lifting hassocks and carrying Tiffany lamps down the basement stairs. Langley had hired men off the street to help out with all this moving, but Siobhan could not let them work unattended—every nick or scrape or floor gouge caused her anguish. To say nothing of the cleaning up and putting everything back afterward.

Langley had gone out and purchased several dozen popular music records so that we would not have to play the same tunes over and over. He had found a music shop over on Sixth Avenue and Forty-third Street, where the Hippodrome theater was located, and the proprietor was a virtual musicologist, with recordings of swing orchestras and crooners and songstresses that no other store had. Our whole idea was to present a dignified social experience for people living hand to mouth. We didn't charge by the dance but asked for a dollar admission per couple—we only admitted couples, no single men, no riffraff looking for women—and for that they got two hours of dancing, cookies and tea, and, for an extra twenty-five cents, a glass of cream sherry. Langley took up his position at the front door every afternoon a few minutes before four, and left an honor plate in the foyer after about ten minutes when most of the people who were coming had arrived. A dollar was not an insignificant amount of money at this time and our customers, many of whom were our neighbors from the side streets off Fifth Avenue and who had once been well off and knew the value of a dollar, came to the tea dance promptly to get the most for their money.

We used three of our public rooms for dancing. Langley handled the turntable in the dining room, I took on the chores in the parlor, and, until Langley figured out how to wire everything with speakers so that one record player could be heard in the three rooms, he hired a man on a day-to-day basis to run things in the drawing room. Mrs. Robileaux tended the sherry bar and held out the salvers of her home-baked cookies to the customers sitting along the walls.

I had learned easily enough to set the record on the turntable without bumbling around and to put the needle in the groove just where it needed to be. I was pleased to be making a contribution. It was a special experience for me to be doing something that people were willing to pay for.

But there were lessons to be learned. Whenever I happened to play one of the livelier numbers, the dancers would leave the floor. Anything fast and happy, and they would sit right down. I would hear the chairs scraping. I said to Langley, The people who come to our tea dance have no fight left in them. They are not interested in having a good time. They come here to hold each other. That's basically what they want to do, hold one another and drift around the room.

How can you be so sure about each and every couple? Langley said. But I had listened to the sound of their dancing. They shuffled about with a sinuous somnolent shushing. They made a strange otherworldly sound. Their preferred music was vaporous and slow, especially as it was played by some bad English swing orchestra with a lot of violins. In fact, what with one thing or another I had come to regard our Tuesday tea dances as occasions for public mourning. Even the Communist who stood at the foot of the front steps to pass out his flyers couldn't rouse up our tea dancers. Langley said he was a little guy, a kid with thick eyeglasses and a pouch full of Marxist tracts. I could hear the fellow—he was a damn nuisance with his abrasive voice. You don't own the sidewalk, he said, the sidewalk is for the people! He wouldn't budge but it didn't matter, he still had no luck handing out his flyers. The couples who came to our dance in their shiny suits and frayed collars, their threadbare coats and limp dresses, were the very capitalist exploiters he wanted to rise up and overthrow themselves.

Only Langley, the ultimate journalist, finally took some of the kid's Communist reading matter, in this case the *Daily Worker*, their newspaper, which you couldn't always find on a newsstand, and the minute he did that the kid apparently felt he'd accomplished his mission, for he strode away and never showed up at another of our tea dances.

Of course they weren't to last that much longer anyway.

THE HEAVY HOUSEWORK that went along with our enterprise was indeed too much for poor Siobhan. When she didn't come down from her room one morning Mrs. Robileaux went up to see what was the matter and found the poor woman dead in her bed, a rosary wound around her fingers.

Siobhan had no relatives that we knew of, and there were no letters in her bureau drawer, nothing to indicate she'd had a life outside our house. But we did find her savings bankbook. Three hundred and fifty dollars, a tidy sum in those days unless you understood these were her life savings after more than thirty years' employment with our family. She did have her church, of course, St. Agnes on the West Side in the Fifties, and they took care of the obsequies for us. The priest there accepted Siobhan's bankbook, whose sums, he said, could be designated for the church's expenses after the State had gone through its usual rigmarole.

By way of atonement Langley placed paid obituaries in every single paper in the city, not only the majors like the *Telegram* and the *Sun* and the *Evening Post* and the *Tribune*, the *Herald*, the *World*, the *Journal*, the *Times*, the *American*, the *News*, and the *Mirror*, but in the *Irish Echo* and the outlying papers, like the *Brooklyn Eagle* and the *Bronx Home News* and even the *Amsterdam News*, for colored folks. To the effect that this good and pious woman had devoted her life to the service of others, and with her simple heart and passion for cleanliness she had enriched the lives of two generations of a grateful family.

But wait—I may be mistaken about the number of newspapers that ran Siobhan's obituary, for by this time the *World* had merged with the *Telegram*, and the *Journal* had combined with the *American* and the *Herald* with the *Tribune*—mergers I remember Langley reporting to me with some satisfaction as early signs of the inevitable contraction of all newspapers to one ultimate edition for all time of one newspaper, namely his.

Ours was the only car behind the hearse in the ride to Queens. We were to bury Siobhan in a vast hill-crawling necropolis of white marble crosses and winged angels cast in cement. Mrs. Robileaux, whom we had taken to calling Grandmamma in the manner of her grandson, Harold, sat in state next to me. For the occasion she wore a mothball-smelling stiff dress that crinkled as she moved and a hat whose broad brim kept slicing into the side of my head. She spoke of her fears for Harold, who was at this time back in New Orleans. He claimed in his letters that he was getting steady work playing the clubs, but she worried that he was making things out better than they really were so that she wouldn't worry.

We were all in a somber mood. With the image of poor Siobhan in my mind, and remembering my trips to the Woodlawn Cemetery to bury my parents, I could only think of how easily people die. And then there was that feeling one gets in a ride to a cemetery trailing a body in a coffin—an impatience with the dead, a longing to be back home where one could get on with the illusion that not death but daily life is the permanent condition.

THE ITEM ABOUT US in the "what to do, where to go" section of one of the evening papers was the first sign of trouble: something to the effect of a high-class taxi dance on Fifth Avenue where you could rub shoulders with the upper crust. We didn't know how the item got there. Langley said, These newspaper people are illiterate—how can one rub shoulders with an upper crust?

At the very next dance we had to close the doors with people still clamoring to get in. Those we had to turn away sat down on the stoop and milled about on the sidewalk. They were noisy. Naturally there followed complaints from the residences south of us: a letter of articulate disapproval, hand-delivered by someone's butler, and an angry phone call from someone who would not give her name, although there may have been more than one phone call from more than one person. Indignation. Umbrage. The neighborhood going to seed. And of course there was the visitation one day of a policeman, though he seemed not to be acting on the complaints of our neighbors. He had his own amiable view of the problem.

Standing at the open door he brought a cold breeze in with him. He announced in rather formal tones that it was against the law to operate a commercial enterprise out of a residence on Fifth Avenue. Then his whiskeyed voice softened: But seeing as you are respectable folks, he said, I am inclined to overlook the matter for a kindly donation of, say, fifteen percent of the weekly monies to the Police Beneficiaries League.

Langley said he had never heard of the Police Beneficiaries League and asked what its work was.

The cop didn't seem to hear. I leave the accounting to you in good faith, Mr. Coller, and I will come by of a Wednesday morning for the remittance and no questions asked, but with a floor of ten dollars.

Langley said: What do you mean "a floor"?

The cop: Well, sir, it would not be worth my time for anything less.

Langley: I understand that criminal matters in this city do press upon your time, Officer. But you see we don't charge much for our tea dances, they are offered more in the nature of a public service. If we have forty couples of an afternoon it's a lot. Add to that our overhead—refreshments, labor costs—and well, we might think about supporting your Police Beneficiaries League with a bribe or, as you call it, a floor of maybe five dollars a week. And for that we would of course expect you to stand out front every Tuesday and touch your cap.

Well now, Mr. Coller, if it was up to me, I would say to you "done and done." But I have my overhead as well.

And that is . . . ?

My sergeant over to the precinct.

Ah yes, Langley said to me, now we're getting to it.

My brother's voice had become raspier. I knew he was toying with the fellow. I thought I would like to take him aside and review the matter, but he was well on his way. Did you really think, he said to the officer, did you really think that the Collyers would give in to a police department shakedown? In my book that's called extortion. So if anyone is breaking the law around here it is you.

The cop tried to interrupt.

You've come to the wrong door, Officer, Langley said. You're a thief, plain and simple, you and your sergeant together. I can respect true bold criminality but not the sly sniveling corruption of your sort. You're a disgrace to the uniform. I would report you to your superiors if they weren't of the same miserable beggarly caste. Now you will get off our property, sir—out, out!

The cop said, You have a sharp tongue, Mr. Coller. But if that's your pleasure I'll be seeing you.

As the cop turned and went down the steps Langley shouted something I will not repeat here and slammed the door.

Langley's exertions had brought on one of his coughing spells. It was difficult to listen to, his wheezing, basso, lung-riddled cough. I went to the kitchen and brought him a glass of water.

When he had calmed down I said to him, That oration was pretty good, Langley. Had a kind of music to it.

I alleged he was a disgrace to his uniform. That was wrong. The uniform is a disgrace.

The cop said he'd be seeing us. I wonder what that meant.

Who cares? Cops are crooks with badges. When they're not taking payoffs, they're beating people up. When they get bored they shoot someone. This is your country, Homer. And for its greater glory I have had my lungs seared.

FOR A WEEK OR TWO, that seemed to be the end of it. Then during one of our dances, there they were, as if that one cop had budded and rebudded until multiples of him were muscling through the rooms and ordering everyone to leave. People didn't understand. In a moment we had a melee—scuffling, shouting, people tripping over one another. Everyone was trying to get out but the police in pushing them, shoving them were intent on creating havoc. The band I had put on the record player moments before kept playing as if in another dimension. How many police there were I don't know. They were loud and bulked up the air. The front door was open and a chill wind blew in off the avenue. I didn't know what to do. The shrieks I heard could have been merriment. With so many bodies in the room, I had the wild idea that the police in all their bulk were dancing with one another. But our poor tea dancers were being driven out the door like cattle. Grandmamma Robileaux had been standing near me with her salver of cookies. I heard a resounding gong, the sound made by a silver salver coming down on a skull. A male yowl and then a rain of cookies, like hail, splattering the floor. I was calm. It seemed to me of utmost importance to stop the music, I removed the record from the turntable and meant to slip it into its jacket when it was grabbed out of my hands and I heard it shatter on the floor. The Victrola was yanked away and heaved against the wall. Without knowing what I was doing—it was instinctive, an animal impulse, like the swat of a bear's paw but something lazier, a sightless man's distraction—I swung my fist through the air and hit something, a shoulder I think, and for my pains received a blow in the solar plexus that sent me to the floor gasping. I heard Langley shout, He's blind, you idiot.

And so ended the weekly tea dance at the Collyer brothers'.

—

WE WERE CHARGED with running a commercial enterprise in an area zoned only for residences, serving alcohol without a license, and resisting arrest. We notified the lawyers who were the executors of our parents' estate. They would act promptly enough but not in time to save us from a night in the Tombs. Grandmamma Robileaux went downtown with us as well to spend the night in the women's detention.

I couldn't sleep—not only because of all the noisy drunks and maniacs in the adjoining cells—I couldn't get over the vindictiveness of the police who had raided the premises as if we were running a Prohibition-era speakeasy. I was outraged that I had been punched and didn't know by whom. There was no way to avenge this. There was no appeal. There was nothing I could do about it except suffer my helplessness. I don't know of a more desolate feeling than that. For the first time in my life I felt the incomplete man. I was in a state of shock.

Langley was calm and reflective, as if it was the most natural thing in the world to be sitting in the Tombs at three in the morning. He said he'd saved a whole box of records from destruction. At that moment I couldn't care less. You go along with the faculties you have almost as if you are normally equipped. And then something like this happens and you realize what a defective you are.

Homer, Langley said, I have a question. Until we began playing records for the dancers, I never really paid much attention to popular songs. But they're powerful little things. They stick in the mind. So what makes a song a song? If you put words to one of your études or preludes or any of those other pieces you like to play, it still wouldn't be a song, would it? Homer, you listening?

A song is usually a very simple tune, I said.

Like a hymn?

Yes.

Like "God Bless America"?

Like that, I said. It has to be simple so that anyone can sing it.

So that's why? Homer? So that's why?

Also it has a fixed rhythm that doesn't change from beginning to end.

You're right! Langley said. I never realized that.

Classical pieces have multiple rhythms.

There is art to the lyrics too, Langley said. The lyrics are almost more interesting than the music. They boil down human emotions to their essence. And they touch on profound things.

Like what?

Well take that song where he says sometimes he's happy sometimes he's blue.

". . . my disposition depends on you."

Yes, well what if she's saying the same thing at the same time?

Who?

The girl, I mean if her disposition depends on him at the same time his disposition depends on her? In that case one of two circumstances would prevail: either they would lock together in an unchanging state of sadness or happiness, in which case life would be unendurable—

That's not good. And what's the other circumstance?

The other circumstance is that if they began disynchronously, and each was dependent on the other's disposition, there would be this constantly alternating mood current running between them, from misery to happiness and back again, so that they would each be driven mad by the emotional instability of the other.

I see.

On the other hand there's that song about the man and his shadow?

"Me and My Shadow."

That's the one. He's walking down the avenue with no one to talk to but his shadow. So there's the opposite problem. Can you imagine a universe like that, with only your own shadow to talk to? That is a song right out of German metaphysics.

At that moment some drunk began to cry and moan. Then other voices began shouting and yelling at him to shut up. Then just as suddenly it was quiet.

Langley, I said. Am I your shadow?

In the darkness I listened. You're my brother, he said.

A WEEK OR SO after our night in jail we went with Grandmamma Robileaux to a hearing in which our lawyers moved to have the charges against us dismissed. As to operating a business in a residential zone they provided Langley's accounts to show that the small profits of each dance were absorbed by the expenses of the dance following so that in a sense it was true that our tea dances were a public service. As to resisting arrest, that charge was only applied to me, a blind man, and Mrs. Robileaux, a stout Negress of grandmotherly age, neither of whom could be reasonably expected, even reacting in fear, to have put up anything which New York's Finest could claim as resistance. The judge said his understanding was that Mrs. Robileaux whacked a serving tray over the head of an arresting officer. Did she deny that? Oh no, Mr. Judge sir, I most certainly don't deny anything I did, Grandmamma said, and I would do it again as a respectable woman to defend myself from the hands of any white devil who would have his way with me. The judge considered this answer with a chuckle. As to the last charge, serving alcoholic beverages without a license, surely a drop of sherry, said our lawyer, could not be seriously considered a crime in this regard. At this point the judge said, Sherry? They served sherry? For goodness' sakes I like a drop of that myself before lunch. And so the charges were dismissed.

IN THE AFTERMATH of the police raid, the house seemed cavernous. The rooms having been emptied for the dance, we had somehow not gotten around to unrolling the rugs, bringing up the furniture, and putting everything back where it belonged. Our footsteps echoed, as if we were in a cave or an underground vault. Though the library still had books on the shelves and the music room still had its pianos, I felt as if we were no longer in the home we had lived in since our childhood, but in a new place, as yet unlived in, with its imprint on our souls still to be determined. Our footsteps echoed through the rooms. And the odor of Langley's stacks of newspapers—they had, like some slow flow of lava, brimmed out of his study to the landing on the second floor—that odor was now apparent, a musty smell that would be especially noticeable on days of rain or dampness. There was a lot of rubble to clean up, all the broken records, smashed phonographs, and so on. Langley treated it all as salvage, inspecting everything for its value—electric cords, turntables, split chair legs, chipped glasses—and filing things according to category in cardboard boxes. This took several days.

Naturally I didn't understand it as such, but this time marked the beginning of our abandonment of the outer world. It was not just the police raid and the neighborhood's negative view of our dances, you understand. Both of us had failed in our relations with women, a specie now in my mind seeming to belong either to Heaven, as my dear unattainable piano student Mary Elizabeth Riordan, or to Hell, as surely was the case of the thieving seductress Julia. I still had hopes of finding someone to love but felt as I had never before that my sightlessness was a physical deformity as likely to drive away a comely woman as would a hunch of the back or a crippled leg. My sense of myself as damaged suggested the wiser course of seclusion as a means of avoiding pain, sorrow, and humiliation. Not that this would be my consistent state of mind, eventually I would rouse myself to discover my true love—as you must know, my dear Jacqueline—but what was gone from me by then was the mental vigor that comes of a natural happiness in finding oneself alive.

Langley had long since reworked his post-war bitterness into an iconoclastic life of the mind. As with the inspiration of the tea dances, he would from now on give full and uninhibited execution to whatever scheme or fancy occurred to him.

Did I mention how vast the dining room had become? A high-ceilinged voluminous rectangle that had always had a hollowness to it, even in the pre-dance days of its Persian rug, its tapestries and sideboards and torch-shaped sconces, its standing lamps and its Empire dining table and eighteen chairs. I had never really liked the dining room, perhaps because it was windowless and situated on the colder north side of the house. Apparently Langley had similar feelings because the dining room was where he elected to install the Model T Ford automobile.

HAVING TAKEN TO MY bed with the grippe, I had no idea what he was up to. I heard these strange noises downstairs— clanking sounds, shouts, metallic shivers, clatterings, and one or two tympanic crashes that shook the walls. He had brought the car in disassembled, the parts hauled up from the backyard by winch and rope, carried through the kitchen, and now being put together in the dining room as if in a garage, into which indeed the dining room was eventually transformed, complete with the smell of motor oil.

I made no attempt to investigate, preferring to compose an image from the sounds I heard as I lay in my bed. I thought it might be some bronzed sculpture, so huge that it came in parts that had to be assembled. An equestrian figuration, for example, such as the statue of General Sherman at the foot of Central Park at Fifty-ninth and Fifth. There were at least two other men's voices, lots of grunting and hammering, and above all my brother's rasp raised to a degree of uncharacteristic excitement verging on joy, so that I knew that here was his new major enterprise.

After a day or two of this Grandmamma Robileaux knocked on my door and before I could say, Come in, she was standing by my bed with a soup of her own prescription. I can smell it now almost as if I was inhaling its spices—a brew thick with okra, turnips, collard greens, rice, and marrowbones, among other ingredients of her arcane knowledge. I sat up in bed and the tray was put across my lap. Thank you, Grandmamma, I said.

I couldn't tuck in because she stood waiting to say something.

Don't tell me, I said.

I knew when he came home from that war your brother's mind weren't right.

That was the last thing I wanted to hear. It's okay, I said. You needn't worry.

No sir, I must dispute that. She sat herself down at the foot of my bed, thus sending the tray into a steep list. I grabbed it and waited for her to continue but I heard only a sigh of resignation as if she was sitting with her head bowed and her hands folded in prayer. Grandmamma had taken to me in a proprietary or even maternal way ever since Harold Robileaux had gone back to New Orleans. Perhaps it was because he and I had played music together, or perhaps for her own sake as the only remaining member of the staff since the death of Siobhan, she needed to find communion with someone in this house. I could understand why Langley was not a candidate.

And now she unburdened herself. Her floor all tracked up with their boots, the back door off its hinges, black mechanical things, auto-mobile things, swinging through the window like clothes on a line. And not just that, she said, that is just the worst. This whole house is dirty and beginning to smell, nobody around to keep it up.

I said: Automobile things?

Maybe you can tell me why that isn't a man out of his mind would bring a street auto-mobile into his house, she said. If it is an auto-mobile.

Well is it or isn't it? I said.

More likely a chariot from Hell. I thank the Lord the Doctor and Miz Collyer are safely in their graves, for this would kill them worse than what did.

She sat there. I could not let her see my astonishment. Don't let it depress you, Grandmamma, I said. My brother is a brilliant man. There is some intelligent purpose behind this, I can assure you.

At that moment of course I hadn't the remotest idea of what it might be.

At this time, the end of the thirties, early forties, cars were *streamlined.* That was the word for the latest up-to-date thing in auto design. Streamlining cars meant warping them, not showing a right angle anywhere. I had made a point of running my hands over cars parked at the curb. The same cars that made purring sounds on the road had long low hoods and sweeping curved fenders, wheel covers and built-in humpbacked trunks. So when I was well enough to come downstairs I said to Langley, If you were going to bring a car into the house, why not a modern up-to-date model?

This was my joke as I sat in the Model T and added exclamation marks with two quick squeezes of the rubber-bulb horn. The honks seemed to bounce around the room and dispense clownish echoes all the way to the top floor.

Langley took my question seriously. This was cheap, just a few dollars, he said. No one wants something this old that has to be cranked up.

Ah, that explains everything. I told Grandmamma Robileaux there was a rational explanation.

Why should this concern her?

She wonders why something from the street has to be in the dining room. Why something made for the outside is inside.

Mrs. Robileaux is a good woman but she should stick to cooking, Langley said. How can you make an ontological distinction between outside and inside? On the basis of staying dry when it rains? Warm when it's cold? What after all can be said about having a roof over your head that is philosophically meaningful? The inside is the outside and the outside is the inside. Call it God's inescapable world.

The truth is that Langley couldn't say why he'd put the Model T in the dining room. I knew how his mind worked: he'd operated from an unthinking impulse, seeing the car on one of his collecting jaunts around town and instantly deciding he must have it while trusting that the reason he found it so valuable would eventually become clear to him. It took a while, though. He was defensive. For days he brought the matter up, though no one else did. He said, You wouldn't think this car was hideous to behold on the street. But here in our elegant dining room its true nature as a monstrosity is apparent.

That was the first step in his thinking. A few days later as we dined one evening at the kitchen table, he said, out of the blue, that this antique car was our family totem. Inasmuch as Grandmamma Robileaux couldn't be more displeased having someone now eating regularly in her kitchen, I understood the remark as something made for her benefit, because presumably, being from New Orleans, a city of primitive beliefs, she would have to respect the principle of symbolic kinship.

All theoretical considerations fell by the wayside the day Langley, having decided our electric bills were outrageous, proposed to set up the Model T's engine as a generator. He ran rubber piping from its exhaust out through a hole he had a man drill in the dining room wall and tied in to the basement wiring board via another hole drilled through the floor. He struggled to get it all working, but succeeded only in making a racket, the running engine and the smell of gasoline together sending Grandmamma and me out the front door one particularly intolerable evening. We sat across the street on a bench at the park wall and Grandmamma announced, as if describing a boxing match, the struggle between Langley and the prevailing darkness, the lights in our windows flickering, sputtering, flaring, and then finally going down for the count. All at once the evening was blessedly quiet. We could not keep from laughing.

Thereafter, the Model T just stood there accumulating dust and cobwebs, and filling up with stacks of newspapers, and various other collectibles. Langley never mentioned it again, nor did I, it was our immovable possession, an inescapable condition of our lives, sunk to its wheel rims but risen from its debris as if unearthed, an industrial mummy.

WE NEEDED SOMEONE to clean house, if only to keep Grandmamma from leaving. Langley fretted about the cost, but I insisted and he finally gave in. We used the same agency that had supplied Julia and we hired the very first people they sent over, a Japanese couple, Mr. and Mrs. Hoshiyama. The reference sheet gave their ages as forty-five and thirty-five. They spoke English, were quiet, businesslike, and totally uninquisitive, accepting everything about our bizarre household. I'd hear them talking as they went about their work, they communicated with each other in Japanese, and it was a lovely music they made, their reedy voices at a third interval, the long vowels punctuated with sharp expulsions of breath. At times I felt myself living in a Japanese wood-block print of the kind on the wall behind the desk in my father's study—the thin tiny cartooned people dwarfed by the snow-covered mountains or making their way under their umbrellas across a wooden bridge in the rain. I attempted to show the Hoshiyamas those prints, which had been there since my childhood, to indicate my judicious approach to ethnicity, but it turned out to be a wrong move, having just the opposite effect I intended. We're American, Mr. Hoshiyama informed me.

The couple needed no instruction, they found things for themselves and what they couldn't find—a mop, a pail, brown soap, whatever it was—they went out and bought with their own money, turning in the sales slips to Langley for reimbursement. Their sense of order was relentless, I would feel a hand on my arm, gently ordering me to rise from my piano bench when it came time to dust the Aeolian. They arrived punctually at eight a.m. every morning and left at six in the evening. Oddly enough, their presence and unflagging industry gave me the illusion that my own days had some purpose. I was always sorry when they departed, as if my animacy was not my own but an allotment of theirs. Langley approved of them for a different reason: they treated his various collections with respect, for instance his hoard of broken toys, model airplanes, lead soldiers, game boards, and so on, some of them whole, some of them not. Langley, once he brought something into the house, didn't bother to do anything with it but throw it in a carton along with everything else he'd found. What they did, the Hoshiyamas, was curate these materials, setting them out on furniture or in bookshelves, these odd jumbles of used and discarded children's things.

So, as I say, we were once again a household up and running though matters were to become complicated once the Second World War began. The Hoshiyamas lived in Brooklyn but one morning they arrived for work in a cab and unloaded several suitcases and a trunk and a bicycle built for two. We heard all this clumping around in the front hall and came downstairs to see what was going on. We are in fear for our lives, Mr. Hoshiyama said, and I heard his wife weeping. The Japanese air force having bombed Pearl Harbor, you see, the Hoshiyamas had been threatened by their neighbors, local merchants refused their patronage, and someone had thrown a brick through their window. We are Nisei! Mrs. Hoshiyama cried, meaning they had been born in the United States, which under the circumstances of course was totally irrelevant. To hear this composed and self-disciplined couple in such states of anguish was unsettling. And so we took them in.

They moved into the room that had been Siobhan's on the top floor and though they wanted to pay rent or at least renegotiate their salaries downward, we would not hear of it. Even Langley, whose miserliness increased exponentially with every passing month, couldn't bring himself to take their money. It astonishes me now to think how well he got along with this couple whose sense of order and cleanliness should have driven him mad. Every evening now there were two shifts at dinner: Grandmamma would serve us and then she and the Hoshiyamas would sit down to their dinner. A diplomatic problem did arise when it turned out that the Hoshiyamas followed a diet not in Grandmamma's realm of expertise and so took to preparing their own food. She said to me she had to turn away the first few times when these people sliced up a raw fish and laid the slices over balls of cooked rice and that was their dinner. Nor could Grandmamma have enjoyed all the traffic in her kitchen, a large high-ceilinged room with its white tiles and open shelves of dinnerware, its butcher-block counters and a big window through which the morning sun shone. This was where she spent most of her waking hours. I said to her, Grandmamma, I know it must be difficult, and she admitted it was, though she felt bad for these people, she knew what it meant to have rocks thrown through your window.

THE WAR WAS BROUGHT home to us in many ways. We were told to buy War Bonds. We were told to save scrap metal and rubber bands, but that was nothing new. Meat was rationed. Draperies had to be pulled across the windows at night. As titular owner of a car, Langley was entitled to a book of gas-ration tickets. He put his "A" sticker on the windshield of the Model T, but having given up the idea of using its engine as a generator, he sold his tickets to a local garage mechanic, a bit of black marketeering which he justified in terms of our financial situation.

Langley's newspaper project seemed to be right in step with what was happening. He read the papers every morning and afternoon in an inflamed state of attention. For good measure we listened to the evening news on the radio. At times I thought my brother took a grim satisfaction from the crisis. Certainly he understood its business opportunities. He contributed to what was called the War Effort by selling off the copper rain gutters and chimney flashing of our house. That gave him the idea of also selling the walnut wood paneling from the library and our father's study. I didn't mind losing the copper gutters but walnut paneling didn't seem to me relevant to the War Effort, and I told him so. He said to me, Homer, many people, general officers for instance, thrive on war. And if some muck-a-muck sitting on his keister in Washington wants walnut paneling for his office, it will be relevant to the War Effort.

I DID NOT REALLY fear for our country though for the first year or so the news was mostly bad. I couldn't believe we and our Allies wouldn't prevail. But I felt completely out of things, of no use to anyone. Even women had gone to war, serving in uniform or replacing their husbands in the factories. What could I do, save the tinfoil from chewing-gum wrappers? These war years found me sinking in my own estimation. The romantic young pianist with the Franz Liszt haircut was long gone. When I wasn't sluggish, I was harshly self-critical as if, no one else noticing that I was a useless appendage, I would warrant that I was. Langley and I disagreed about this war. He didn't see it in the same patriotic terms, his view was Olympian, he scorned the very idea of it apart from who was right and who was wrong. Was this a lingering effect of the mustard gas? War to his mind was only the most obvious indication of the fatal human insufficiency. But there were specifics to this Second World War, where evil could justifiably be assigned, and I thought his contrarian attitude was misguided. Of course, we didn't argue, it was a characteristic of our family, going back to our parents, that if we disagreed with each other about a political matter, we simply avoided talking about it.

When Langley went out on his nightly forays, I sometimes played the piano till he got back. The Hoshiyamas were my audience. They brought up two straight chairs and sat behind me and listened. They were familiar with the classical repertoire and would ask me if I knew this Schubert or that Brahms. I would play for them as if they represented a full house at Carnegie Hall. Having their attention brought my spirit out of the doldrums. I found myself particularly responsive to Mrs. Hoshiyama, who was younger than her husband. Though they spoke Japanese as they worked it was clear to me that he directed her. I wouldn't ask to touch her face, of course, but my sense of her was of a trim little being with bright eyes. I listened as she walked about—she took very feminine, short, shuffling steps and I decided that she was pigeon-toed. When husband and wife worked together in one of the rooms and talked their Japanese talk, I would hear her laugh, probably at something of Langley's newly acquired on one of his nightly rambles. Her laughter was lovely, the melodic trill of a young girl. Every time I heard it, there in our cavernous house, images of a sun-filled meadow flashed in my mind, and if I looked hard enough I could see us, Mrs. Hoshiyama and me, as a kimonoed couple in a wood-block print having a picnic under a cherry blossom tree.

When the three of us were together in the evening and the for-
mality of our daytime relationship was suspended, I felt that it
was only my deep respect for Mr. Hoshiyama that prevented me
from stealing his wife. On such gentle fantasies do men like me
survive.

ONE NIGHT, WITH LANGLEY out for the evening, the bell
rang and there was at the same time a peremptory knock on the
door. It was quite late. Two men who said they were from the
FBI were standing there. I felt their badges. They were polite
and though they were already in the door they asked if they
could come in. They were there to take the Hoshiyamas into
custody. I was stunned. I demanded to know why. What is this
about, I said. Has the couple done something illegal? Not that
we know, said one of the men. Have they broken the law in any
way? Not that we know, said the other. You will have to give me
a good reason why this is happening, I said, they work for me.
They are my employees. These are simple hard-working people,
I said. They have served me well and honestly and had come to
me, furthermore, with excellent references.

Of course I was an idiot about all of this, but I could think of
no other way to forestall what was happening than by bringing
up anything I could to break through the intolerable stubborn-
ness of these FBIs, who were uncommunicative and impervious
to reason. You come here in the night to take people away as if
this is some police state? I wanted them to feel ashamed of

themselves, which was of course impossible. When men like this are carrying out government policies they are hard-shelled and cannot even be insulted. They are doing something that might seem momentous and horrifying to the people they have come for but is mere routine for them.

They did say one thing by way of justification: that they had gone to the couple's Brooklyn domicile only to learn that the Hoshiyamas had fled. And as a result some effort was required to trace them. At this I flew into a fury. These people were not running away, I said. For their own safety they had to leave their home. They were being physically threatened. Did they even know you were looking for them? And now you are finding something guilty about the fact that they came here to avoid getting their heads bashed in?

I don't remember how long I carried on this way but at some point Mr. Hoshiyama was touching my arm in a mute appeal for restraint. The Hoshiyamas were born fatalists. It was as if they and the FBI men seemed to understand one another so as to make me and everything I said irrelevant. They did not themselves protest, nor cry nor bemoan the situation. After a while Mrs. Hoshiyama came down the stairs with two valises, all they were allowed to bring with them. The couple put on their hats and coats—it was the winter of the first year of the war—the FBI men opened the door and a cold wind blew in from the park. Mr. Hoshiyama mumbled his gratitude and said they would write when and if they could and Mrs. Hoshiyama took my hands and kissed them, and they were gone.

—

WHEN LANGLEY CAME home later that night and heard what had happened he was furious. Of course he knew what it was all about having read in his newspapers of the roundup of thousands of Japanese-American citizens for internment in concentration camps. Though I had told him that Mr. Hoshiyama had opened the door and that the agents asked if they could come in when they were already inside, my ineffectiveness, or stupidity, was demonstrated even so. This house is our inviolate realm, Langley said. I don't care what kind of damn badge they flash. You kick them out and slam the door in their faces, is what you do. These people ignore the Constitution whenever they so choose. Tell me, Homer, how we are free if it's only at their sufferance?

So for a day or two I did feel as Langley felt about warmaking: your enemy brought out your dormant primal instincts, he lit up the primitive circuits of your brain.

LANGLEY AND I treasured the couple's bicycle built for two, which they'd been forced to leave behind. It had an honored place under the stairs. I said we should ride it to keep it toned up for when the Hoshiyamas returned. And so we got into the habit of taking the bike out when the weather was fine.

I was much cheered by pedaling away. It was good to be getting some exercise. I had moments of doubt with Langley steering because he could be distracted seeing something of interest in the street or in a store window. But this only added to the derring-do. We rode in and out of the side streets and took pleasure from the horns that blew behind us. This activity went on for one whole spring until a tire blew as we cut a corner too closely. Langley's strategy for repairing the tire was to replace it. In wartime you could not find anything new that was made of rubber, so for a while he picked up secondhand bikes here or there to see if he could get a tire match. He never did, and the bicycle built for two has stood ever since on its handlebars in the parlor and with a few other bikes propped against the wall to keep it company.

The Hoshiyamas also left their collection of little ivory carvings—ivory elephants and tigers and lions, monkeys hanging from branches, ivory children, boys with knobby knees, girls with their arms round one another, ladies in kimonos and samurai warriors with headbands. None of the pieces was bigger than one's thumb, all together it was a Lilliputian world amazingly detailed, revelatory to the touch.

We will save all their things for when they come back, Langley said, though they never did and I don't know now where any of the little ivory carvings are—buried somewhere under everything else.

And so do people pass out of one's life and all you can remember of them is their humanity, a poor fitful thing of no dominion, like your own.

OUR FRONT DOOR seemed to be a wartime attraction. We found ourselves answering to the knock of old men in black.

They spoke with accents so thick we couldn't quite understand what they were saying. Langley said they were bearded and had curls of hair around their ears. Also dark haunted eyes and rueful smiles of apology for disturbing us. They were very religious Jews, we knew that much. They showed their credentials from various seminaries and schools. They held out tin boxes with slots in which we were asked to put money. This happened three or four times over the course of a month and we began to be annoyed. We were uncomprehending. Langley thought we should post a plaque next to the door: Beggars Not Welcome.

But they were not beggars. One morning it was a clean-shaven man who stood at the open door. He would be described to me as having close-cropped gray hair and a Victory Medal from the Great War pinned to the lapel of his suit jacket. He sported one of those skullcaps on his head that meant he too was Jewish. The man's name was Alan Roses. My brother, who had a soft spot for anyone who had served in that war, invited him in.

It turned out that Alan Roses and Langley had been with the same division in the Argonne forest. They talked as men do who discover a military kinship. I had to listen to them identify their battalions and companies and recall their experiences under fire. It was a completely different Langley in these exchanges— someone who accorded respect and received it in return.

Alan Roses told us what the mystery was with these door-to-door appeals. It had to do with what was happening to Jews in Germany and Eastern Europe. The idea was to buy freedom for Jewish families—Nazi officials were happy to use their racial policies as a means of extortion—and also to inform the American public. If the public was aroused the government would have to do something. He was very calm, and spoke in great and telling detail, Alan Roses. He was, by profession, an English teacher in the public school system. He cleared his throat often as if to swallow his emotion. I had no doubt that what he was saying was true, but it was at the same time so shocking as almost to demand not to be believed. Langley said to me afterward: How is it those old men who knocked on our door knew more than the news organizations?

It was difficult under the circumstances for Langley to maintain his philosophical neutrality. He quickly wrote out a check. Alan Roses provided a receipt on the stationery of an East Side synagogue. We went to the door with him, he shook our hands, and he left. I supposed he would find another door to knock on and subject himself to more embarrassment—he had the reticence of someone doing something out of principle for which he was ill-equipped by nature.

With each day's papers, Langley searched the news columns. The story was coming out on the back pages in dribs and drabs with no appreciation of the enormity of the horror. This went right along, he said, with our government's do-nothing policy. Even in war, deals are made, and if they can't be made you bomb the trains, disrupt the operation—anything to give those people a fighting chance. Do you suppose this land of the free and home of the brave is just not that crazy about Jews? Of course the Nazis are monstrous thugs. But what are we if we let them go ahead and do what they do? And what happens then,

Homer, to your war story of good versus evil? Christ, what I wouldn't give to be something other than a human being.

LANGLEY'S CONTRARIANISM was to evolve. How could it not? When we learned that Harold Robileaux had joined up—this was sometime later, I don't remember what year of the war this was—we displayed one of those little blue-star pennants that people hung in their windows to indicate that we had a family member in the service. Harold had gone and applied to the Army Air Forces and been trained as an airplane mechanic, this musician of all sorts of gifts and capabilities, and by the time we knew any of this he was overseas with an all-Negro pursuit squadron.

So now our spirits were lifted, we were as prideful as any family in the neighborhood. For the first time in this war I felt a part of things. The times had brought people together and in this cold city of impassive strangers where everyone was out for himself a sense of community was like a surprisingly warm spring day in the middle of winter, even though it took a war to do that. I would go out for a stroll—I used a cane now—and people would greet me or shake my hand or ask if they could help me, under the impression that I had been blinded fighting for my country. "Here, soldier, let me give you a hand." I didn't think I looked that young but maybe I was perceived as an officer of formerly high rank. Langley exchanged greetings with home guards from the neighborhood on their way to the rooftops of their buildings to scan the sky for enemy planes. He bought War Bonds on our behalf, although I have to say not purely from patriotism but because he believed they were sound investments. There may have been a European battlefront and a Pacific front, but we were the Home Front, as important to the War Effort, as we canned the vegetables from our victory gardens, as G.I. Joe himself.

Of course we knew there was a powerful propaganda machine behind all of this. It was calling on us to tamp down the fear of the maleficent enemy that resided in our hearts. I would go to the movies with Grandmamma just to hear the newsreels—the boom of our battleship guns, our grinding tank treads, our roaring flights of bombers taking off from English airfields. She would go in hopes of seeing Harold sitting in an airplane hut and looking up from one of the engines he was fixing to smile at her.

We had no victory garden, our backyard had been given over to storage—things accumulated over the years that we had bought or salvaged in expectation of their possible usefulness sometime in the future: an old refrigerator, boxes of plumbing joints and pipes, milk-bottle crates, bedsprings, headboards, a baby carriage with missing wheels, several broken umbrellas, a worn-out chaise longue, a real fire hydrant, automobile tires, stacks of roof shingles, odd pieces of lumber, and so on. In an earlier time I had enjoyed sitting in that little yard where a shaft of sunlight visited briefly toward noon. There was some sort of weed tree there that I liked to think of as an offshoot of Central Park, but I was happy to give up the yard just to get some of these things out of the house because every room was becoming a kind of obstacle course for me. I was losing my ability to sense where things were. I was no longer the young man with the infallible antennae who could blithely circumnavigate the household. The Hoshiyamas when they were with us had brought up furniture from the basement with every intention of restoring things as they had been, but of course that was impossible, everything was different now. I was like a traveler who had lost his map, Langley couldn't have cared less where anything went, and so the Hoshiyamas had used their own judgment and, as well meaning as they were, inevitably had gotten things wrong, which only added to the confusion.

Oh Lord, and then one terrible day, the phone rang and it was this tiny tearful girl's voice, barely audible. She was Ella Robileaux, Harold's wife, calling long-distance from New Orleans, and she wanted to speak with his Grandmamma. I hadn't known Harold had married. I knew nothing about it, but I had no reason to doubt her identity, this child of the tremulous voice, and it took me a moment to collect myself, for I understood without being told why she was calling. When I shouted back to the kitchen for Grandmamma to come to the phone my voice broke and a sob escaped from my throat. This was wartime, you see, and people didn't make expensive long-distance calls just to chat.

BEFORE HE WAS shipped overseas, Harold Robileaux had made one of those little Victory records that soldiers sent home in the mail so their family could hear their voice. Little three-

minute recordings on scratchable plastic records the size of a
saucer. Apparently there were these recording studios in the
same penny arcades near the army bases where you got four
photos for a quarter or a bearded mechanical fakir in a glass case
would lift his hand and smile and send your printed fortune out
of a slot. So Harold had sent Grandmamma his V-record
though it took some months to reach us. Until Langley thought
to check the postmark it was unnerving to have found something from Harold in our mailbox. You understand this was
after Grandmamma had heard from Ella Robileaux that
Harold had been killed in North Africa. Perhaps the army cen-
sors had to listen to every one of these V-records just as they
read every letter the soldiers wrote, or perhaps the post office in
Tuskegee was overwhelmed. In any case when this record arrived in the mail Grandmamma thought Harold was alive after
all. Thank you, Jesus, thank you, she said, crying for joy. She
clapped her hands together and praised the Lord and would not
hear from us anything about a postmark. We sat with her in
front of the big Victrola and heard him. It was a tinny-
sounding record but at the same time it was Harold Robileaux,
all right. He was well, he said, and excited to have been pro-
moted to tech sergeant. He couldn't tell us where he was going
or when but he would write when he got there. In that soft New
Orleans lilt, he said he trusted that Grandmamma was well and
to please give his regards to Mr. Homer and Mr. Langley. It was
all what you'd expect from any soldier in the circumstance,
nothing unusual, except, being Harold, he had his cornet with
him. And being Harold, he put it to his lips and played taps as

if offering the musical equivalent of a photograph of himself in uniform. The quality of that cornet's sound overcame the primitive nature of the recording. A clear pure heartbreaking sound, every phrase lifted to its unhurried perfection. But why did he play the elegiac taps rather than, say, reveille, to indicate his affiliation with the army? Grandmamma asked Langley to play the record over, and then again three or four more times, and though we didn't have the heart to discourage her, maybe it was that solemnly reflective dirge, the mournful tones filling all our rooms over and over, as if Harold Robileaux was prophesying his own death, that made her admit to herself, after all, that her grandson was gone. The poor woman, having been made to suffer his death twice, could not control her tears. God, she cried, that was my blessed boy you took, that was my Harold.

Langley went out and bought gold-star pennants for the front windows of all four storeys, gold being the star for soldiers who had made what the politicians called "the ultimate sacrifice," there being presumably a sequence of sacrifices a soldier could make—arms, legs?—before the ultimate one. Usually a single pennant with one star of blue or gold in a window was enough advertisement or consolation for a household, but Langley never did anything like everyone else. My brother's sorrow was indistinguishable from rage. With the death of Harold Robileaux his whole attitude toward the war had changed and he said that when he finally prepared the front-page war dispatches for his eternally current and always up-to-date newspaper, its advocacy would be explicit. I look at all these papers, he said, and they may come at you from the right or the left or the muddled middle but they are inevitably of a place, they are set like stone in a location that they insist is the center of the universe. They are presumptively, arrogantly local, and at the same time nationally bullish. So that is what I will be. Collyer's One Edition for All Time will not be for Berlin, or Tokyo, or even London. I will see the universe from right here just like all these rags. And the rest of the world can go on with their dim-witted daily editions, whereas without their knowing it, they and all their readers everywhere will have been fixed in amber.

GRANDMAMMA'S GRIEF FILLED the house. It was silent, monumental. Our condolences were met with indifference. One morning she announced that she was leaving our employ. She intended to go to New Orleans and find Harold's widow, whom she did not know, a young girl, she said, who might need her help. Apparently an infant child was involved. Grandmamma was resolute and it was clear to us that these were relationships she would foster, putting together what was left of her family.

The day of Grandmamma's departure she made breakfast for us in her traveling clothes and then washed the dishes. She was taking a Greyhound bus from the terminal on Thirty-fourth Street. Langley pressed traveling money upon her, which she accepted with a regal nod. We stood on the sidewalk as Langley waved for a cab. I was reminded of the day we stood here like this to say goodbye to Mary Elizabeth Riordan. There were no tears and no parting words from Grandmamma as she got into the cab. Her mind was already under way. And so as she rode off the last member of our household was gone, and Langley and I were left to ourselves.

Grandmamma had been the last connection to our past. I had understood her as some referent moral authority to whom we paid no heed, but by whose judgments we measured our waywardness.

WHEN THE WAR ENDED with the victory over Japan it was one of those oppressively close August days in New York. Not that anyone minded. Cars paraded along Fifth Avenue, drivers blowing their horns and shouting out the windows. We stood at the top of our stoop like generals taking review, because people were running by as closely as in ranks, thousands of footsteps scuttling downtown looking for the party. I had listened to the same excitement, the laughter, the running feet like the whir of birds' wings, on Armistice Day 1918. Langley and I crossing the street to the park found strangers dancing with one another, ice cream vendors tossing Popsicles to the crowds, balloon sellers letting go their inventory. Unleashed dogs ran in circles, barking and yelping and getting underfoot. People were laughing and crying. The joy rising from the city filled the sky like a melodious wind, like a celestial oratorio.

Of course I was as relieved as anyone that the war was over. But underneath all this gaiety I found myself in an awful sadness. What was the recompense for the ones who had died? Memorial days? In my mind I heard taps.

We had a joke, Langley and I: Someone dying asks if there is life after death. Yes, comes the answer, only not yours.

WHILE THE WAR WAS on I had come to feel my life was purposeful, if only in its expectations for the future. But with peace I found there was no future, certainly not in any way to distinguish it from the past. In the light of naked truth I was a severely disabled man who could not expect for himself even the most normal and modest of lives—for instance, as a working man, a husband, and a father. This was a bad time in the midst of everyone's joy. Even my music had lost its appeal. I was restless, slept poorly, and in fact was often afraid to go to sleep, as if to sleep was to put on one of the gas masks Langley had brought home in which I could not hope to breathe.

Have I not mentioned the gas masks? During the war he'd acquired a crateful. He saw to it that two were hung on nails in every room of the house so that wherever we happened to be, if the Axis powers did attack New York, and gas bombs were dropped, we were prepared. Given his lifelong cough and shredded vocal cords, his company having been without masks in 1918 when the fog rolled in, I did not demur. But he insisted that I practice putting on a mask so that when and if the time came I would not die fumbling around. To have my nose and mouth covered in addition to being in the dark was frightening. It was as if the sense of smell and taste, too, were being taken from me. I found it hard to breathe through the canister, which meant I could avoid dying of poison gas only by dying of suffocation. But I made the best of it and did not complain, even though I thought a German gas attack on Fifth Avenue highly unlikely.

By the time of war's end, the productive might of the American economy having overproduced everything a soldier would need, we'd collected, besides the gas masks, enough military surplus to outfit an army of our own. Langley said G.I. stuff was so cheap in the flea markets that it presented a business opportunity. We had ammunition belts, boots, helmets, canteens, tin food containers with tin utensils, telegraph keys, or "bugs," developed for the Army Signal Corps, a tabletop full of olive drab trousers and Ike jackets, uniform fatigues, hard wool blankets, pocketknives, binoculars, boxes of service ribbons, and so on. It was as if the times blew through our house like a wind, and these were the things deposited here by the winds of war. Langley never did work out the details of any business opportunity. So along with everything else, all these helmets, boots, etc. ended up now where they had been deposited, artifacts of some enthusiasms of the past, almost as if we were a museum, though with our riches as yet uncataloged, the curating still to come.

Not everything would go to waste—when our clothes wore out we would take to wearing fatigues, both trousers and shirts. And boots too, when our shoes fell apart.

Oh, and the oiled M1 rifle that had never been fired. This was one of my brother's prize acquisitions. Fortunately he hadn't found the cartridges to go with it. He drilled a heavy nail into the marble mantel and we hung up the M1 by its shoulder strap. He fancied his work so well that he did the same for the Springfield rifle that had been sitting there for almost thirty years. They dangled over the fireplace, the two rifles, like Christmas stockings. We never touched them again and though at this point I cannot get anywhere near the mantel, so far as I know they are still there.

I SHOULD MAKE it clear that I did not wish for another war to lift my spirits. It seemed like just a few moments since V-J Day—that's what the victory over Japan was called—and we were at it again. I thought how foolish we had all been that day of delirious celebration, the whole city shouting its joy to the heavens.

When I played piano for the silent movies the picture would end and the projectionist would stick his head out of the booth. The next feature will begin shortly, he'd say. A moment, please, while we change reels.

And so there we were at war in Korea, but, as if we needed something of more substance, we and the Russians were racing to build bigger nuclear bombs than the bombs dropped on Japan. Endless numbers of them—to drop on each other. I should have thought just a couple of superbombs to char the continents and boil the seas and suck up all the air would be sufficient to the purpose, but apparently not.

Langley had seen a photograph of the second atom bomb that had been used on Japan. A fat ugly thing, he said, not sleek and sharklike as you would expect a respectable bomb to be.

You'd think it was something to hold beer. The moment he said that I remembered the empty kegs and ponies he had brought into the house from a brewery that had gone out of business. He lugged these aluminum barrels up to the front door, somehow lost control, and they bounced down the stone steps clanking and booming and rolling across the sidewalk so that I now thought of the atom bomb as an implodable beer keg, lying on its side and spinning on its axis until it decided to go off.

The trouble with listening to the news with Langley was that he became agitated, he raved and ranted, he talked back to the radio. Langley, as an expert newspaper reader, reading all the papers every day, knew what was going on around the world better than the commentators. We'd listen to some commentator and then I'd have to listen to Langley commentating. He would tell me things I knew were true but which nevertheless I didn't want to hear, all of it just adding to my depression. Eventually, he would stop giving me his political insights, which boiled down anyway to a hope that there would soon be a nuclear world war in which the human race would extinguish itself, to the great relief of God . . . who would thank Himself and maybe turn His talents to creating a more enlightened form of creature on a fresh new planet somewhere.

Whatever the news of the world, with Grandmamma Robileaux gone we were faced with the practical problem of how to feed ourselves. Homer, said my brother, we will take our meals out, and it will do you good to be up and about instead of sitting in a chair all day and feeling sorry for yourself.

We had our breakfast at a counter place on Lexington Avenue, a brisk ten- or twelve-minute walk. I'm just thinking a moment about the food: they served fresh orange juice, eggs any style with ham or bacon, hash brown potatoes, toast, and coffee for a dollar and a quarter. I usually had my eggs as an omelet sandwich on the toast as that was easy to handle. For a breakfast it wasn't cheap but other places charged even more. For dinner we went to an Italian place on Second Avenue, a twenty-minute walk. They had various spaghetti dishes, or entrées of veal and chicken, chopped salad, and so on. It wasn't very good but the owner saved the same table for us every night and we brought our own bottle of Chianti and so it was passable. We skipped lunch entirely, but in the afternoon Langley would boil water and we'd have tea with some crackers.

But then he toted up the month's dining bills and, forgetting he had prescribed our eating out as a way of improving my state of mind, he decided to cook at home. He sought at first to duplicate the restaurant meals we had had for breakfast and dinner. But I would smell things burning and weave my way to the kitchen, where he was cursing and tossing hot and hissing frying pans into the sink, or I would sit patiently at the table long past the usual dinner hour, starving and in suspense, until something unnameable was laid before me. Langley asked me one day why I supposed I was looking so peaked and thin. I didn't say, How else should I look given the culinary experiences I have endured? Finally, he gave up and we began to eat out of cans, though he had decided that oatmeal was an essential constituent of good health and put up a batch of the gluey stuff for breakfast every morning.

It would take some time before his interest in healthful eating expanded and he would turn his attention to my blindness as something curable via nutrition.

WHAT LANGLEY DID by way of cheering me up was to buy us a television set. I did not even try to understand his reasoning.

These were the early days of television. I touched the glass screen—it was square with rounded sides. Think of it as pictorial radio, he said. You don't have to see the picture. Just listen. You're not missing anything: what is static on a radio is like it's snowing on the TV. And when the picture does clear, it tends to float up off the screen only to rise again from the bottom.

If I was not missing anything why bother with it? But I sat there in the interest of science.

Langley was right about the relation to radio. Television shows were structured like radio programs, coming in half-hour segments, or sometimes even whole hours, and with the same daytime soap operas, the same comedians, the same swing bands, and the same stupid advertising. There was not much point to my listening to television unless it was a news broadcast or a game show. The news was all about Communist spies and their worldwide conspiracy to destroy us. That was hardly cheering, but the game shows on television were another matter. We got into the habit of tuning them in mostly to see if we could answer the questions before the contestants did. And we were able to do that quite often. I knew the answer to almost anything having to do with classical music and, because of my time playing records for the tea dances, I'd come up with a fair guess or two about popular music. And I was pretty good with baseball and literature. Langley knew history and philosophy and science to a fare-thee-well. Who was the first historian, the quizmaster asked. Herodotus! said Langley. And when the contestant was slow to answer, Langley shouted, Herodotus, you idiot! as if the fellow might hear him. That made me laugh and so it became our habit to call those people on the shows idiots. How far was the sun from the earth? Ninety-three million miles, you idiot! Who wrote *Moby-Dick*? Melville, you idiot! And even when a contestant happened to come up with the right answer, listening, say, to the opening phrase of Beethoven's Fifth—Da-da-da-dum, the same three shorts and a long that in Morse code meant the V, which made it a popular piece during the war—and saying the composer was Beethoven, we'd shout, Good for you, you idiot!

Given our success rate with these game shows, we naturally considered offering ourselves as contestants. Langley did a little research as to how to go about it. Apparently there was a great demand for slots on these shows, and why not, as there was money to be made. One sent in a C.V. and had interviews and background checks, just as if the show was produced by the FBI. We gave ourselves a test listening to one half-hour show and we broke the bank. The trouble was, Langley said, that we were too smart. There would be no suspense. And Homer, these contestants who come on smiling like fools, they are an embarrassment. When they win something, they jump up and down like marionettes on a string. Would it be worth the money to you to carry on like that? No? I said. I agree, he said. It's a matter of self-respect.

And so we chose not to proceed. Of course I had some idea at the time that we were not sartorially typecast. He had told me the men predictably wore flannel suits and rep ties and crew cuts and women down-to-the-ankle skirts and blouses with big collars and bangy hairdos. Langley, who was now bald on top, had let the gray hair on the back of his head grow down to his shoulders. My own Lisztian fall from its center part was considerably thinned out. And our preferred dress was army greens and boots, leaving to the moths in the closets our old suits and blazers. We couldn't have gotten past the front door.

CHRIST, IF THERE was ever an invention nobody needed, Langley said. By then we had another couple of TVs that he had found somewhere. None of them had worked to his satisfaction.

When you read or listen to the radio, he said, you see the scene in your mind. It's like you with life, Homer. Infinite perspectives, endless horizons. But the TV screen flattens everything, it compresses the world, to say nothing of one's mind. If I watch any more I'd might as well take a boat down the Amazon and have my head shrunken by the Jivaro.

Who are the Jivaro?

They are this jungle tribe that likes to shrink heads. It's their custom.

Where did you hear that?

Read it somewhere. After you decapitate the guy you make a slit from top of the head down the back of the neck and then peel the whole thing off the skull—neck, scalp, and face. Sew it into a pouch, stitch up eyelids and lips, fill it with stones, and boil the damn thing down till it's the size of a baseball.

What does one do with a shrunken head?

Hang it by a hair along with the others. Tiny human heads in a row swinging gently in the breeze.

Good Lord.

Yes. Think of the American people watching television.

BUT BEFORE WE unplugged the TV forever, it happened that they were televising the hearings of a Senate committee investigating organized crime. Let's just look at that, Langley said, and so we tuned in.

Senator, a witness was saying, it's no secret that in my youth I was a wild kid, and I grew up the hard way, meaning I did time. That juvenile rap is like a dead bird around my neck and so you subpoeny me here.

Are you denying, sir, that you are the head of New York's leading crime family?

I am a good American and I sit down with you because I got nothing to hide. I pay my taxes, I go to church every Sunday, and I give to the Police Athletic League, where they keep kids playin' ball and out of trouble.

Good God, I said, do you realize who that is? It must be! I'd recognize that voice anywhere.

If it is he's heavier, Langley said. Dressed like a banker. Most of his hair's gone. I'm not sure.

Who doesn't change in twenty-five years? No, it's him. Listen to that: How many gangsters speak in a whisper with an attached wheeze in high C? That's Vincent all right. He asked me how it felt to be blind. And now he's at the top of his profession. He's a big muck-a-muck in front of a Senate committee. He sent us champagne and girls, I said. And then we never heard from him again.

Did you hope to?

I was being idiotic, I know, carrying on about this hoodlum. I wasn't the only one. I don't remember what he actually testified to but after his appearance the tabloids were all over him. I had Langley read to me: "Vincent Rats!" they screamed in their headlines as if it was they who'd been betrayed. And then their accounts of the rackets he was alleged to be running, his competitors who had mysteriously died, the various courtroom trials from which he'd emerged with an innocent verdict, thus affirming a guilt so vast that the law could not get around it, and, what was most suspenseful, the arch enemies he was reputed to have made among the other crime families. I was very impressed.

Langley, I said, what if we had been a crime family? How

much closer we would have been to Mother and Father if we had all worked together running protection rackets, gambling syndicates, loaning money to people at exorbitant rates, committing every imaginable felony including murder though I think not prostitution.

Probably not prostitution, Langley said.

AFTER THE SENATE HEARINGS, Langley had pulled the plug and thrown the TV set into a corner somewhere, and we were not to look at television again until a decade later when the astronauts landed on the moon. I never told my brother that in my own way I could see the television screen: I saw it as an oblong blur just a shade lighter than the prevailing darkness. I imagined it as the eye of an oracle looking into our house.

My thrill at having once met a famous gangster was indicative of how bored I was by my own life. When, a few weeks later, a news bulletin came over the radio that Vincent had been shot while dining in an East Side restaurant, it was a weird pride I felt—the sense of being a privileged insider, an I-knew-him-when feeling that was quite insensitive to the extremity of his situation. After all, I was a fellow who sat most of the day in his house, living without the normal complement of friends and associates, and with no practical enterprise to occupy his days, a man with nothing to show for his life but an overworked consciousness of it—who can blame me for acting like a fool?

It was that testimony he gave, I said to Langley. The crime

families don't like publicity. The Mayor feels pressure to do something, the D.A. gets busy and the cops start pulling them in.

All at once, you see, I was the expert criminologist.

I waited by the radio. Diners had seen Vincent being carried to his limo and driven away. Was he alive or dead? I was left with a vague sense of expectation. That is something less than a premonition but can be just as unsettling. Jacqueline, when you read this, if you do, you might think, Yes, at this point of their lives poor Homer was losing his mind. But forget the oracular power I imputed to a TV set and you are left with an improbability that had a certain logic to it. I think now what happened I had wanted to happen, though what I will describe here was finally only one more passing event in our lives—as if our house were not our house but a road on which Langley and I were traveling like pilgrims.

WHEN THE PHONE RANG I was sitting by the table radio in our father's study. I was startled. Nobody ever called us. Langley had gone to his room to type the day's news précis for his filing system. He came running downstairs. The phone was in the front hall. I answered. A man's voice said, Is this the archdiocese? I said, No this is the Collyer residence. And the line went dead. The archdiocese? Maybe a minute later there was a pounding at the door. You understand this was a barrage of loud sudden sounds, a ringing phone, a pounding at the door, that rendered us totally responsive. When we opened the door three men barged in carrying another under the arms and legs, and that was the actual Vincent, whose outflung arm knocked me aside, and left a wet streak on my shirt that turned out to be his blood.

What interests me—I discussed this many times with Langley over the years—was why we stood at the open door as these killers came past us, and instead of leaving the house to them and running off to find the police we responded dutifully to their shouts and orders, shutting the door and following them where they bumblingly wandered with Vincent howling when they stumbled over things, to settle in my father's study, where amid the books and the shelves of bottled fetuses and pickled organs they sat him down in an armchair.

We were curious, Langley said.

One of the trio of henchmen would turn out to be Vincent's son. Massimo, his name was. He had been the voice on the phone. The other two were the same men who had driven us home from the nightclub so many years before. I would never hear them speak more than a word or two, usually mumbled. I thought of them as granitelike—hard, verging on inanimate. Vincent's left ear had been shot away and lest whoever was after him could finish the job—a cartel of New York crime families, if I had judged right—one of the granite men had remembered our house and, perhaps after driving around desperately looking for someplace to hole up, had realized nothing was more unlikely for the pursuit to imagine than a residence on Fifth Avenue, and so found our phone number to see if we were still in residence (as opposed to the archdiocese?) and voilà, there we were, a newly designated safe house for a famous criminal bleeding from what remained of his ear.

—

WITH THEIR BOSS deposited in the chair, and Massimo kneeling beside him and holding a bloodied restaurant napkin to the afflicted ear, the gangsters seemed unable to think further what must be done. There was this silence except for the soft moaning of Vincent, who, I must say, was totally unconnected in my mind to the man of my memory. There was none of the cool suave self-assurance that I remembered and that I expected of him now. It was disappointing. Possibly a bullet tearing off a chunk of ear might have left him with tinnitus, but really it was a minor wound in terms of what is essential to life. So his problem was no more than cosmetic. Do something, he muttered, do something. But his men, perhaps stunned by the array of our father's collection of human organs and fetuses floating in jars of formaldehyde, the tons of books spilling artfully out of the shelves, the old wooden skis in the corner, the side chairs piled one on top of another, the flowerpots filled with the earth of my mother's botany experiments, the Chinese amphora, the grandfather clock, the innards of two pianos, the tall electric fans, the several valises and a steamer trunk, the stacks of newspapers piled in the corners and on the desk, the old cracked black leather medical bag with the stethoscope hanging out of it—all of it evidence of life well lived—as I say, in the face of all this the men seemed unable to move. It was Langley who took charge, assessing the nature of Vincent's wound and finding in a drawer of my father's desk right there rolls of gauze, adhesive tape, cotton balls, and a bottle of iodine, which he judged to be at its maximum potency given the years of its aging.

Vincent's yowls as he was treated apparently alerted his men for I felt something pressed under my ribs that I assumed was a gun barrel. But the critical moment passed—Here, I heard Langley say, wrap this around his head—and in short order the yowls had given way to a reprised moan.

THE MEN RECONNOITERED and decided to bring their boss into the kitchen. Upstairs he might be caught like a rat in a trap. The kitchen, being closest to the back door, offered a fast escape in the event pursuit came up the front steps. They brought down from Siobhan's old room her mattress and two pillows. So there, propped on what had been Grandmamma Robileaux's big, thick-planked, turned-leg farm table—I remember my mother had wanted a country look in the kitchen—was our celebrity criminal, petulant, self-pitying, demanding, and—heedless of the presence of strangers—abusive to his son.

Massimo seemed to have the rank of a gangster in training and nothing he did was right according to his father: if he wanted to summon the family doctor, that was stupid, if he ran out for cigarettes or something to eat, he was too goddamn slow. Massimo didn't look like his father, or like I remembered his father: he was a roly-poly fellow and entirely bald with a rotund head and an ample double chin, as I suspected even before we were chummy enough for him to let me trace his features, and altogether unfortunate for a fellow not yet thirty. I would find myself trying to make him feel not so bad. Your father is in pain, I said, and doesn't deal well with it. It's no different than always, said Massimo.

I remember thinking that as a replacement for his father Massimo would never make the grade. I was wrong, though. Some years later, when Vincent was finally shot to death, Massimo became the head of that crime family and was even more feared than his father had been.

WE WERE BROUGHT into the kitchen when Vincent had calmed down enough to have a look at us. It was like being given an audience. Who are these people, he said with his whistly voice. Street bums looking for a handout? Massimo said, They live here, Pop. It's their place. Don't tell me, Vincent said. They got hair like they never seen a barber. And this one staring into space like some doper. Oh I see, he's blind. Jesus, what comes out of the woodwork in this town. Get 'em outa here, I got enough troubles without having to look at these cretins.

I was shocked. Should I have told Vincent that we had met some years before? But that would have been to affirm my humiliation. I felt like a fool. As with any celebrity or politician, the man was your best friend until the next time around when he has no recollection of ever having met you. Langley being present had the good grace never after to remind me of my idiocy.

—

WE WERE TO HAVE our houseguests for four days. Pistols were trained on us just at the beginning. I wasn't afraid and Langley wasn't afraid either. He was furious to the point where I was sure that he would burst a blood vessel. Massimo, on orders of his father, tried to pull the phone cord out of the wall. It wouldn't give. Langley said, Here, I'll do it for you, we have no use for the damn thing, never have. And he yanked on the phone so hard that I heard pieces of plaster coming out of the wall with it and then he flung the whole thing across the study and broke the glass on one of our father's bookcases.

My brother and I had to stay at all times where we could be seen. If we left the room, one of the thugs had to go with us. By the second day, this vigilance relaxed and Langley simply went back to his newspaper project, and in fact was helped in this by the men, who took turns going out in the morning and evening to pick up the papers so as to see what was being said about the shooting and Vincent's disappearance.

The men were dumbfounded by the state of the hideaway they had chosen. They couldn't understand the absence of a recognizable means of sitting down anywhere. In their minds we were a household given to strange otherworldly furnishings— like the stacks of old newspapers in most of the rooms and on the stair landings. But when they came upon the Model T in the dining room, if it had been up to them they would have departed immediately. It may be that their bewilderment is what saved us from harm, for I heard them talking among themselves as to how glad they would be to escape from this place—*madhouse,* I think, is the word they used.

HERE I SHOULD mention the typewriters. Sometime before this, Langley had decided he needed a typewriter to begin to bring order to his master project, the single newspaper for all time. He first tried the one our father had used. It sat on the Doctor's desk—an L. C. Smith Number 2. It wasn't the engreased dust that bothered Langley, but that the ribbon was dried out and the keys required great pressure of the fingers. I think even if he had found the machine to be in perfect order Langley would have gone out, as he eventually did, to find some others because, as in all such matters, one would not do where an assortment might be had. Consequently after a while a battery of machines were in our possession—a Royal, a Remington, an Hermès, an Underwood, among the standard models, and, because he was delighted to locate it, a Smith-Corona that had been fitted with keys in Braille. That is the one I'm using now. So for a while, as Langley worked his way through the imperfections of each of the machines, there was a new music in my ears of key clacks and bell dings and slamming platens. I was surprised that he eventually found a model to satisfy him. The rest were accorded museum status, untended and forgotten, like everything else, with the exception of one beauty he found in a shop in the West Forties, a very old Blickensderfer Number 5, which felt to my touch like a metallic butterfly with its wiry wings in full flight. This was given an honored place on the washstand in his bedroom.

As the third day came around with no sign of Vincent's departure—he slept most of the time—my brother and I slowly went back to the daily routine of our lives with no interference from the gangsters, and this bizarre situation took on a semblance of normality. Langley typed away on his project and I resumed my daily practice sessions at the piano. It was as if two separate households were sharing the same space. They brought in their food and we took care of ourselves, though after a while we ran out of most everything we had in the pantry and they began to leave things for us. Their cuisine came in white cardboard boxes and was quite good—Italian specialties brought in at night—theirs was a one-meal regimen—and in return we made coffee in the mornings and sat with them on the steps to the second floor. When Vincent awoke, he proceeded to complain from his kitchen bed and demand and curse and threaten everyone in sight. He turned us all into a kind of oppressed fraternity, he'd become a universal burden, and so finally there was a sort of bonding—the two brothers and the three hoodlums.

I should have thought his men preferred Vincent asleep to Vincent awake but they were increasingly nervous as they waited fitfully for their next orders. They wanted to know now what retaliation lay in store. They wanted to know what was to be done.

ON THE FOURTH MORNING I heard a terrible crash. It had come from the kitchen. The men ran in there. I followed. There was no sign of Vincent.

They kicked open the pantry door and found him cowering in the corner. You hear that? Vincent said. You hear that?

I heard it, we all heard it. The men were on alert now, their guns drawn, one of them prodding me in the ribs. Because there it was, the rat-a-tat of something relentlessly mechanical, like the deadly sputter of a tommy gun. Vincent had fallen or rolled off his makeshift kitchen bed having been startled awake by that sound, presumably familiar to him in his long life of crime. This was a delicate moment and I knew if I laughed it would be the end of me. I merely pointed at the ceiling and let them work it out for themselves that it was Langley at his typewriter, Langley being a very fast typist, his fingers racing to keep up with his thoughts, and his room located directly overhead. What typewriter he was using I didn't know—the Remington, the Royal, or perhaps the Blickensderfer Number 5? He had set it up on a fold-out card table that was not quite steady and the clacking keys as transmitted through the spindly legs of the table, and through the floor, picked up a darker hammering tone that, I suppose, if you were a sleeping gangster who had recently been shot at, could have sounded like another attempt on your life.

Vincent, recovering his poise, laughed as if he found it funny. And when he laughed so did the others. But he'd been shocked into a state of aggressive awareness. No more sleeping now, he was the crime boss once again.

What is this dump! he said. Am I in a junkyard? This is what you guys find for me? Massimo, the best you can do? Look at this place. I have retribution to think of. I have serious matters.

And you drop me in this rat's nest. Me! And where is the intelligence I need, where is the information I count on? I see you look at each other. You wanna give me excuses? Oh there are debts to pay, and I will pay them. And when I've put out their lights I will turn to who in the family set me up. Or shall I believe it's blind fate that I am now minus one ear. I'm talking to you! Is that what it was, blind fate, they just happened to find me in the restaurant where I was?

His men knew better than to say anything. They may have even been comforted to find their boss up to form. I could hear him striding about, pushing things out of the way, throwing things aside.

AS LANGLEY TOLD ME later it was as Vincent prowled about holding a hand over his ear hole that he found one of the army surplus helmets and put it on. And then there was a need to see himself in a mirror and the men brought down the standing mirror from my mother's bedroom, a lady's bedroom mirror that could tilt in its frame.

As Vincent saw his reflection he realized his suit was a mess. He stripped—off came the jacket, trousers, shirt—and in his skivvies and shoes and socks he found a set of our army fatigues that fit him and said, Nobody will believe this is me in this outfit. I could walk out the front door in broad daylight. Hey, Massimo, whaddya think? I look like anyone you know?

No, Pop, the son said.

A course I can't be seen like this. What it would do to my rep. He laughed. On the other hand if I'da had on this helmet the other night I'd still have my ear.

Our washing machine was in the alcove behind the kitchen, an old model with a wringer attached, and one of the men found it and took Vincent's clothes and dropped them in the machine to get all the bloodstains out. We must have had by then a good number of electric irons and two or three antique hand irons that you put on the stove to get them hot. So some time went by as Massimo and one of the men attempted to get Vincent's suit washed and wrung out and ironed so that it was a reasonable simulation of a dry-cleaned suit.

While all this was going on Langley didn't see why he should stand there and be bored so he went back upstairs to his typewriter and the clacking and platen banging resumed and Vincent said, Massimo, go up there and tell the old man he doesn't shut up with the typewriter I'll stick his hands in this clothes wringer. Massimo, showing an initiative in an effort to please his father, brought the typewriter down in his arms and Vincent took it and heaved it across the room and I heard it come apart with a silvery shatter, like a piece of china.

IT WAS ONLY WHEN Vincent was preparing to leave that I became frightened. I wanted him gone but what might he order his men to do to us by way of parting? For hours it seemed, the crime family consulted among themselves while Langley and I waited, as instructed, upstairs.

When the last light had faded from the windows we were summoned and tied up in two kitchen chairs back-to-back with clothesline, of which we happened to have enough looped and coiled in the hardware cabinet in the basement to go twice around a city block, though our practice in hanging things to dry was to prefer those metal umbrella rigs, of which we had a few, that could be unfolded and folded again when we were through with them, because Langley had imagined that I would forget a clothesline was strung out somewhere in the house and accidentally garrote myself.

You will never say a word, Vincent said. You will keep your mouths shut or we will come back and shut them for you.

And then I heard the front door slam and they were gone.

All was silent. We sat there tightly bound, back-to-back, in our kitchen chairs. I heard the ticking of the kitchen clock.

BEING TIED UP AND unable to move leads one to reflect. The fact was that thugs had broken into our home and taken it over and not once had we offered any resistance.

We had befriended the family, sitting with them and having coffee, I feeling sorry for Massimo—but how was that anything but propitiation? The more I thought about it the worse I felt. At no time did they consider us worth shooting.

The rope around my arms and chest seemed to be tightening with my every breath. I was ashamed, furious with myself. We could have played some kind of trick, suggested that Vincent was dying. These morons wouldn't have known the difference. I might have persuaded them to let me leave and find a doctor.

I listened to the ticking of the kitchen clock. A sense of the futility of life rose in my gorge as an overwhelming despair. Here we were, the Collyer brothers, totally humiliated, absolutely helpless.

And then Langley cleared his throat and spoke as follows. I remember what he said as if it was yesterday:

Homer, you were too young at the time to be aware of it, but one summer our mother and father took us to a kind of religious resort on a lake somewhere upstate. We lived in a Victorian manse with wraparound porches on the first and second floors. And in the whole community every house was like that—Victorians with shade porches and cupolas and rocking chairs on the porches. And each house was painted a different color. Does any of this ring a bell? No? People got around on bicycles. Every morning began with a prayer breakfast in the community dining room. Every afternoon there were merry sing-alongs led by a banjo band of men in straw boaters and red-and-white-striped jackets. "Down by the Old Mill Stream." "Heart of My Heart." "You Are My Sunshine." The children were kept busy—potato-sack races, classes in raffia weaving and soap carving—and down at the lake the community fire engine had the nozzle of its water cannon aimed at the sky so that we could run under the spray shrieking and laughing. Every afternoon with the sun beginning to set over the hills a paddle steamer came down the lake with hoots and whistles. In the evenings there were concerts or lectures on worthy subjects. Everyone was happy. Everyone was friendly. You couldn't walk a few steps without being greeted with big smiles. And I tell you, I had never in my young life been so terrified. Because what could the purpose of such a place be but to persuade people that this was what Heaven would be like? What other purpose than to give an inkling of the joys of eternal life? I was young enough to think there was such a thing as Heaven . . . to imagine myself spending eternity with the banjo band in their straw boaters and striped jackets, to think I might someday be stuck there among all these imbecilic happy people praying and singing and being educated in worthy subjects. And to see my own parents embracing this hideously unproblematic existence, this life of continuous and unrelenting happiness so as to indoctrinate me to a life of virtue? Homer, that dismal summer is when I realized our mother and father would inevitably fail all my expectations of them. And I made a vow: I would do whatever it might take to avoid going to Heaven. Only when, just a few years later, it became clear to me that there was no Heaven was a heavy weight lifted from my shoulders. Why do I tell you this? I tell you this because to be a man in this world is to face the hard real life of awful circumstance, to know there is only life and death and such varieties of human torment as to confound any such personage as God. And so that is affirmed here, isn't it? To find the Collyer brothers tied up, helpless and humiliated by a vulgar brute? This is one of life's own speechless sermons, isn't it? And if God is there after all, we should thank Him for reminding us of His hideous creation and dispelling any residual hope we might have had for an afterlife of fatuitous happiness in His presence.

Langley was always able to lift my dark moods from me.

ALL RIGHT, I SAID, then this is just something else to deal with. Let's get to it.

We were tied to the ladder-back Shaker chairs with rush seats that were my mother's choice to go with the big farm table that Vincent had used as a bed, itself an outrage as I thought about it. It was no use struggling against the clothesline webbed and knotted round our arms and in and out of the back slats. But I had noticed that the legs of my chair wobbled a bit as I moved from side to side. These chairs are older than we are, I said.

Right, Langley said. When I say three, throw yourself to the left. We'll go down. Watch your head.

And so that's what we did—heaved ourselves over and when we crashed to the floor the back of my chair broke apart and suddenly the clothesline was loose enough for me to twist around and slip out of the loops and untie Langley.

There was great satisfaction in accomplishing this maneuver. We staggered to our feet, brushed ourselves off, and shook hands.

THIS WAS IN THE early autumn of the year. It was still quite warm, and so by way of enjoying our liberation we went out and sat on the bench directly across the street under the old tree whose branches reached out over the park wall. It felt good to be outside. Even the fumes of a passing Fifth Avenue bus smelled good. I heard some birdsong, then someone walking a dog, a big dog by the clicking sound of its paws on the pavement. I sat back on the bench and tilted my face toward the sky. Never had normal ordinary life in the out-of-doors been so delicious.

Langley appraised the condition of our house. The lintels over the second-floor windows, he said. Chipped away here and there. And the cornice, chunks of it missing. I don't know when that happened. And there's some sort of filthy bird's nest tucked in one of the gaps. Well why not birds, he said. Home to the world. Thieving servants, government agents, crime families, wives . . .

Only one wife, I said.

One's enough.

We discussed going to the police but of course we would never do that. Self-reliance, Langley said, quoting the great American philosopher Ralph Waldo Emerson. We don't need help from anyone. We will keep our own counsel. And defend ourselves. We've got to stand up to the world—we're not free if it's at someone else's sufferance.

And so we sat there for some time in philosophical reflection and let the shock of the experience wear away in the warm autumn afternoon with Central Park at our backs and the image of its composed natural green world filling my mind.

WHEN WE WERE tied up in those chairs Vincent had crumpled up a couple of hundred-dollar bills and thrown them down at

Langley's feet, like to a beggar. I thought we used the money well by ordering in from a lumber supply house heavy louvered shutters custom fitted to the front windows. Langley had them painted black. We also had the front door bolted with steel brackets and a two-by-four cross brace. This would encourage us to ask who was there before we opened the door.

But the shutters seemed to be a signal of some significance to the real estate profession. Brokers were drawn to our house as birds to a feeder. Their knockings on the door and presumptuously cheerful hellos became a daily occurrence. Most of the time they were women. And when we stopped answering they took to dropping their cards and brochures through the mail slot. And then someone, probably one of those same real estate agents, had tried to phone us and, receiving a perpetually busy number, reported that to the phone company. And so telephone repairmen appeared, and there were further poundings on the door and shouts from us that we didn't want any. Since the day Langley had ripped the phone out, neither of us had felt the need to be reconnected. And even as the phone company should have known from their repair department that the phone was already out of service, they sent letters threatening to disconnect us if we didn't pay the ever increasing past-due bills. Langley thanked them, saying we were already disconnected but eventually we had to deal with a collection agency, the first of several representing creditors with whom Langley's battles were to achieve a kind of notoriety.

My brother and I conferred. He had understood my uneasiness with the perpetual darkness in the house. You would think that wouldn't matter to me, but I had found myself gravitating to the back rooms, whose windows still looked out. I could tell daylight from darkness by the varying temperatures or even by scent, darkness smelling one way and light another. So I had not been entirely happy with our self-reliance. My Aeolian didn't like the darkness either, its tonal quality seemed to have changed, it was more muted, less declarative, as if it had found itself muffled in the gloom.

And so, what with one thing and another, we threw open the shutters and, for a while, we would again be windowed on the world.

LANGLEY GOT ME in his sights and decided I looked flabby. You're getting soft, Homer, and that does not bode well for good health. He dug out the Hoshiyamas' tandem bicycle with its flat tire and bolted it to frames that lifted the wheels off the ground so that I could pedal away and not go anywhere at the same time. And every morning we took a brisk walk down Fifth Avenue and back on Madison Avenue and once around the block for good measure. Of course that was just the beginning of his campaign. He had brought home a nudist magazine that was fervent in its advocacy of radical health regimens. Not that we were to go about without clothes, but that, for instance, heavy doses of vitamins A through E reinforced with herbs and certain ground nuts found only in Mongolia might not only ensure long life but even reverse pathological conditions such as cancer and blindness. So now I found at the breakfast table, beside the usual bowl of viscous oatmeal, handfuls of capsules and nuts and powdered leaves of one kind or another, which I dutifully swallowed to no appreciable affect as far as I could determine.

I should say that there was nothing wrong with me—I felt fine, never better in fact, and I didn't mind the exercise at all—but not wanting to hurt my brother's feelings I went along with this dietary nonsense. Besides which I was moved by his concern for my welfare. That I was become one of his projects pleased me in some way.

Among his collectibles that I had come across in the parlor was a bas-relief of a woman's head that he'd hung from a nail on the wall. It was like a large cameo. I felt her features, the nose, the forehead, the chin, the waves in her hair, and it gave me tactile pleasure to run my fingers over this raised half face even as I knew the piece was of no great value, a reproduction perhaps of something hanging in a museum somewhere. But Langley had seen me, and it must have been on this occasion that he was inspired to do something about my woeful deprivation as a person to whom the fine arts were inaccessible.

At first he brought in from his wanderings some miniature bone ivory netsuke carvings of Oriental couples making love. They were of the same proportions as the miniature ivories that the Hoshiyamas had left behind but we couldn't have found those even if we had looked. I was invited to feel these small depictions of sexual bliss and figure out just what intricate positions the pairs of tiny heedless lovers had gotten themselves into. There were also masks of smooth-faced plaster of Paris creatures, and fearsome African deities carved from wood, that he had picked up at some flea market or auction. So in this manner what I called Langley's Museum of Fine Arts began to distinguish itself from everything else of the inanimate world that, over the years, we had come to live with. And I was now engaged in a course of tactile art appreciation. But this wasn't art for art's sake: Langley had read up on the anatomy and pathology of the eye in our father's medical library. Rods and cones are what make the eye see, he told me. They're the basis of everything. And if a damn lizard can grow a new tail why can't a human being grow new rods and cones?

So just like my breakfast of Mongolian ground nuts, my course in art appreciation was a means of restoring my sight. It's a one-two punch, Langley said. Herbal restoratives from the inside and physical training from the outside. You have the material for rods and cones and you train your body to grow them from the fingers on up.

I knew better than to protest. Each morning I squinted my eyes into the morning light to see if things were any different. And each morning Langley waited for my report. It was always the same.

After a while I grew irritable. Langley counseled patience— It'll take time, he said.

There was a week with children's finger paints, those little tubs of dyed glop, which he had me smearing over sheets of paper to find out if I could learn to tell the color by touch. Of course I couldn't. I felt degraded by the exercise. Another scheme had me going about the house and running my hands over paintings that I remembered from when I could still see: Horses on the bridle path in Central Park. A clipper ship at sea in a storm. My father's portrait. That portrait of my mother's great-aunt who had ridden a camel across the Sudan for no reason that anyone could determine. And so on. The worst part of this assignment was getting to the walls. Twice I tripped and fell. Langley had to move things, throw them out of the way. I knew each painting by its placement, but visualizing it by touch was another matter, I felt only brushstrokes and dust.

None of this made much sense to me. I was beginning to feel oppressed. Then one day Langley opened the door for a delivery of art supplies—canvases stretched on frames of various sizes, a big wooden easel, and boxes of oil paints and brushes. And now I was to play the piano while he painted what he heard. The theory was that his painting would be an act of translation. I was not to play pieces, I was to improvise and the resulting canvas would be the translation to the visual of what I had rendered in sound. Presumably, when the paint dried, in some synaptic flash of realization, I would see sound, or hear paint, and the rods and cones would begin to sprout and glow with life.

I considered the possibility that my brother was insane. I wished heartily that he would go back to his newspapers. I played my heart out. Never since I had first lost my sight had I felt so deprived, so incomplete as I felt now. The more he tried to improve things for me, the more aware I became of my disability. And so I played.

I should have known that, having taken up art on my behalf,

Langley would devolve into an obsessive amateur artist with all thoughts of my reclamation put aside. What did I know if I didn't know my brother? I had only to wait. He did not limit himself to oil paints for his compositions, but attached to the canvas any manner of things as the spirit moved him. Found objects he called them, and to find them he needed only to look around, our house being the source of the bird feathers, string, bolts of cloth, small toys, fragments of glass, scraps of wood, newspaper headlines, and everything else that inspired him. Presumably he was making the work as tactile as he could for my sake, but really because dimensionality pleased him. Breaking rules pleased him. Why after all did a painting have to be flat? He would plant a canvas in front of me and have me touch it. What is the subject, I would say and he would answer, There is no subject, this piece does not represent anything. It is itself and that's enough.

How blessed were these days in which Langley had half forgotten why he had taken up painting. I would hear him at his easel, smoking and coughing, and I would smell the smoke of his cigarettes and his oil paints, and I would feel like myself again. Somehow those episodes in which he'd had me improvising on the piano had left me with an awakened sense of my possibilities as a composer, and so now I was improvising to forms—working up études, ballades, sonatinas and, being unable to write them down, fixing them in my memory. Langley in the other room understood what was going on with me because he went out and brought back a wire recording machine, and then, later, a couple of improved machines that recorded on tape, and so I was able to listen to myself and make changes, and think of new themes and record them before they got away from me, and I felt that neither of the Collyer brothers had ever been happier than at this time.

My brother's canvases from those days are stacked against the walls, some of them in our father's study, some in the front hall, some in the dining room with the Model T. Some he hung on the staircase wall leading to the second and third floors. I can still smell the oils even after all this time. The recordings I made are somewhere in the house, buried under God knows what. My venture into composing was a finite thing, as was his life as a painter, but it would still be interesting, were I able to look for those tapes, those spools of wire, just to hear what I had done. I envision unwound tapes lying entangled among everything else, besides which I would not know where to look for the machines to play them. And finally my hearing . . . my hearing is not what it used to be, as if this sense too has begun to retreat to the realm of my eyes. I am grateful to have this typewriter, and the reams of paper beside my chair, as the world has shuttered slowly closed, intending to leave me only my consciousness.

BUT NOW I WILL mention Langley's last painting—the last one he did before he went back to his newspapers. It was inspired not by the astronauts' first flight to the moon, but by their subsequent commutes. He had me touch it. I felt a sandy surface embedded with rocks and cratered with mounds of what seemed to be some sort of sanded epoxy glue. I wondered if he had reverted to representation, for I thought it felt much like the moon would feel if I bent down to touch it. But it was a huge canvas, the largest he had done, and as I moved my hand about, I found adhered to the surface some sort of stick, and as I moved my hand down along this stick it became thinner and suddenly veered into a right-angled chunk of metal. What is this, I said, it feels like a golf club. That's what it is, Langley said. And then at other places on the canvas small books had been affixed by the spine and individual pages, stiff with glue, were sticking up as if blown by the wind—three or four of these in various sizes. Is there wind on the moon? I said. There is now, my brother said.

I thought the moon painting wasn't very good—I had no trouble visualizing it, was the problem. Perhaps Langley realized it was a failure because that was the last one he did. Or maybe it was those moon walks of our astronauts that made Langley give up painting as insufficient to his rage. Can you imagine the crassness of it, hitting golf balls on the moon? he said. And that other one, reading the Bible to the universe as he circled around out there? The entire class of blasphemies is in those two acts, he said. The one stupidly irreverent, the other stupidly presumptuous.

For my part, I was awestruck, and I said to him, Langley, this is almost unimaginable, going to the moon, it is like some dream, it is astounding. I would forgive those astronauts whatever they did.

He wasn't having any of it. I'll tell you the good news about this space venture, Homer. The good news is that the earth is finished, or why would we be doing this? There is a great sub-liminal species perception that we are going to blow up the planet with our nuclear wars and must prepare to leave. The bad news is that if we do in fact get off the earth we will contami-nate the rest of the universe with our moral insufficiency.

If that is the case, I said, what will happen to your eternal always up-to-date newspaper?

You're right, he said, I must make room for a new category—technological achievement.

But technological achievements succeed one another—which one could stand for all?

Ah my brother, don't you see? The ultimate technological achievement will be escaping from the mess we've made. There will be none after that because we will reproduce everything that we did on earth, we'll go through the whole sequence all over again somewhere else, and people will read my paper as prophecy, and know that having gotten off one planet, they will be able to destroy another with confidence.

I'M RECALLING NOW that tale of Quasimodo, the hunchback of Notre Dame—this poor defective and how he loved a beau-tiful girl and would ring the great cathedral bells in his an-guished passion. In my longing for a lover I wondered if that was me. Or could I, after all, find some woman who would take up with me from some genius of her own loving spirit. The model I had in mind for this person was Mary Elizabeth Rior-dan, my piano student of yore. Actually it was Mary Elizabeth

Riordan herself I wished for. I had kept my feelings for her as one keeps a precious object hidden away in a box. I fantasized that someday she would return to us a grown young woman newly sensitive to the history of my diffident and formerly imperceptible courtship. It was a cruel coincidence or malign alignment of spiritual forces that even as I was thinking of her she was writing to us for the first time in many years.

Langley brought her letter in from the front hall. It had come slipped into the usual packet of bills, lawyers' letters of warning, and Building Department notices that the mailman always thoughtfully bound with a rubber band. Well look at this, Langley said. A Belgian Congo stamp. Who is Sr. M. E. Riordan?

My God, I said, is that my piano student?

Her long silence was explained: she had taken vows, she was a sister in some worthy order. She was a nun! Dear friends, I know I should have written before this, I heard her say in Langley's voice, but I hope you will forgive me.

Dear friends? What had happened to Uncle Homer and Uncle Langley? People didn't just take vows, they took dictions. I asked Langley to read the letter over again: Dear friends, I know I should have written before this, but I hope you will forgive me and pray for these poor people who I am privileged to serve.

She explained that in her order the sisters were missioners, they went around the world where the people were poorest and most miserable and they lived among them and tended to them.

I am in this impoverished and drought-ridden country living

in a village among the poor and oppressed, she wrote. Just last week army troops came through and killed several of the men of the village for no reason at all. These people are poor farmers wresting their food crops out of a harsh rocky hillside. Two of my sisters are here with me. We provide what sustenance and medicine and solace we can. I feel blessed by God in my work. The only thing I miss is a piano and I pray for the Lord to forgive me for this weakness. But sometimes in the evening when they have one of their village ceremonies, they bring out their hand drums and sing, and I sing with them.

I had Langley read the letter to me for several days running. I was trying to acclimate. The children are undernourished, she wrote, and they get sick a lot. We are trying to start a small school for them. Nobody here knows how to read. I ask my God why in some places people can be so poor and wretched and uneducated and yet love Jesus with a purity that transcends whatever might be possible in New York, a city so far away just now, so heedless, that huge city where I grew up.

It is a shameful thing to confess but, with the news of what Mary Elizabeth Riordan had done with her life, I felt betrayed. Her passion was for others, countless others, it was a dispensed passion, a love for anyone and everyone, whereas I wanted it to be for me. In all these years had she ever thought of me? I could match in neediness any broken-down indigent of the Congo. And if things were so godless in New York, what better place for a missioner?

The sister had enclosed a photograph of herself and some

little children in front of what looked to be the village church. It is not much more than a stone hut with a cross over the door, Langley said. And she looks different.

How so?

This is a mature woman. Maybe it's because she's wearing a sun hat. You see just her hairline and her face. She looks heavier than I remember.

Good, I said.

Nor is the letter that of a girl. This is a grown woman talking. How old do you suppose she is?

I don't want to hear it, I said.

Past fifty, I should think. But isn't it interesting that someone in the grip of such a monstrous religious fantasy—believing she is doing the Lord's work—is doing the work that the Lord would be doing if there was a Lord?

I could not be as philosophical as Langley about my sweet girl's chosen life. I will not here detail the lascivious proposals of my imagination, the arch seductions that I composed at night from my memory of her slight figure, the modest indications of her form in the simple dresses she wore, or from the touch of her hand on my arm as we strode to the movie theater where she told me what was on the screen. The lips and eyes I had traced with my fingertips I now kissed, and from the shoulder that had brushed mine as we sat together at the piano I now let loose the strap of her shift. This went on for some nights, she in her shy acquiescence and I gently but firmly teaching her her pleasure and seeing to the conception of our child. How sad that I was reduced to these expedients till all my anguish was dissolved in futility and the tactile image of what had been Mary Elizabeth Riordan had faded from my mind.

I don't know how Langley truly felt about her letter. He would rather hide behind some philosophical bon mot than reveal what love he had kept for the girl. It would not be in character for my brother to identify with Quasimodo. But it happened that the next period of our lives saw an uncharacteristic sociability akin to recklessness on both our parts, as we opened our house to the strange breed of citizen now springing up around the country. If there was a thin edge of bitterness to what we were doing, if we were moving as far away as we could from the saintliness of Mary Elizabeth Riordan, disinheriting her in our minds and consigning ourselves to hellish reality by looking for her replacement, we were not conscious of it.

Of course that another damnable war had sprung up was enough to strip away any residual inhibitions I may have had. Was this country unexceptional after all? I was at this point in my life as close in spirit to Langley's philosophical despair as I had ever been.

WHAT HAPPENED WAS that an antiwar rally was held in Central Park on the Great Lawn and we thought we'd have a look at it. We could hear it long before we got there, the sound of the hoarse loudspeakered voice throbbing in my ears though the words were indistinct, and then the cheers, a flatter broader unamplified sound, as if the speaker and the audience were in different realms—a mountaintop, perhaps, and a valley. And the blurred oration again for a line or two and the cheers again. This was early in October of that year. It was a warm afternoon, with an autumnal light that I felt on my face. You will say that was the warmth of the sun I felt, but it was the light. It lay on my eyelids, it was the golden light of the low quarter that comes with the dying of the year.

We stood at the edge of the crowd and listened to a folk music group performing a song in earnest praise of peace with that willed naïveté that goes along with such music. The audience joined in at the chorus and that turned out to be the last of it, there was a round of cheers by way of conclusion, and people began to file past us on their way out of the park.

Not everyone was willing to give up the occasion, among them Langley. We wandered among the groups sitting on the grass, or on lawn chairs, or blankets, and I was stunned to hear my brother exchanging pleasantries with strangers. An oddly convivial feeling came over me. The Collyers—principled separatists, recluses—and here we were, just two more of the crowd. And I don't quite remember how it happened, but some young people there welcomed us into their company and what with one thing or another we were soon sitting with them on the Great Lawn and taking swigs from their wine bottles and breathing the fine acrid scent of their marijuana cigarettes.

I realized later that it was our dress, our comportment that these children responded to. Our hair was long, Langley wore his like a tied horse tail down the back, and I just let mine fall over the sides of my head to my shoulders. And our clothes were casual to the point of dereliction. We had on our old boots and Levi's, we wore our work shirts and holey sweaters under well-used and torn-at-the-elbows jackets that Langley had picked up at a flea market, and from these garments our new friends were persuaded that we were of their way of life.

By the time it drew dark, police came driving their cruisers there on the grass, running their sirens at a low growl, nudging people to their feet, telling us all to move on. Our new friends simply assumed they were to come home with us and we didn't even make a point of acquiescing, as that would have been in bad form. It was as if—without knowing any of them or which of them belonged to which name—we'd been inducted into a relaxed and sophisticated fellowship, an advanced society, where ordinary proprieties were *square*. That was one of their words. Also *crash*, meaning, as I was to learn, boarding with us. We'd been recognized, is how I felt, as did Langley I could tell, as if with an honorific. And when these children—there were five who peeled off from the larger group and walked up the steps into our house, two males and three females—saw of what a warehouse of precious acquisitions it was comprised, they were moved beyond measure. I listened to their silence and it seemed to me churchlike. They stood in awe in the dim light of the dining room looking upon our Model T on its sunken tires and with the cobwebs of years draped over it like an intricate netting of cat's cradles, and one of the girls, Lissy—the one I was to bond with—Lissy said, Oh wow! and I considered the possibility, after drinking too much of their bad wine, that my brother and I were, willy-nilly and ipso facto, prophets of a new age.

—

IT TOOK ME A DAY or two to sort them all out. I call them children, though of course they weren't really. Eighteen or nineteen, on average, and one of them, JoJo, the heavyset bearded one, was twenty-three, though his age didn't give him any privileged status. He was in fact the most childlike of them all, a fellow given to buffoonery and laughingly tall tales which you were not expected to believe. JoJo turned serious only when he sat down to smoke, marijuana putting him in a philosophical state of mind. Brotherhood was his theme. He called everyone, whatever their gender, "man." When you refused his offer of a toke it was as if you had delivered a fatal wound. Ah, man, he would say, his grief inexpressible, ah, man. Unlike Connor, the other male, he didn't seem to be romantically attached to any of the girls, perhaps because of his weight. I had known fellows like him at school, who, given their girth, chose to be no more than boon companions to the ladies. But it was JoJo who would, in time, work like a stevedore to bale Langley's newspapers and set up the labyrinthian pathways of those impacted blocklike bales according to Langley's instructions.

Connor, or Con, was monosyllabic and from what I could infer a cadaverous figure with a long neck and thick eyeglasses. He wore no shirt but a denim jacket open over his hairless torso. He spent his time drawing comic strips in which men's feet and women's breasts and behinds were greatly exaggerated. Langley told me the strips were quite good in their appalling way. A touch surreal, he said. They seemed to celebrate life as a

lascivious dream. I asked Connor what he intended in his draw-
ings. Dunno, he replied. He was quite busy, having cleared out
a place for himself in a corner of the music room, and setting
himself up at an antique schoolroom desk my mother had gotten for me when I was too small to go to real school.

Two of the girls—Dawn and Sundown were their chosen
names—hovered over Connor utterly transfixed by the obscene
adventures of his characters. Of course he had modeled his
busty females after them. One day Langley told me that Connor had incorporated us as well into his strips. Ah the ruthless-
ness of art that consumes the world and everyone in it, he said.
What do we look like, I said. What is he having us do? We are
old gray-haired lechers with little heads with bulging eyes and
buck teeth and our legs get wider as they reach the ankles and
our feet are fitted with enormous shoes, Langley said. We like
to dance with our index fingers pointing to the sky. We pinch
ladies' bottoms and hold them upside down so that their dresses
fall over their heads. How insightful, I said. I'm going to buy
these strips when he's finished with them, Langley said. Muse-
ums will bid for them one day.

Langley told me Dawn and Sundown were nice but had not
much going in the way of thought. They wore long skirts with
boots, and fringed jackets, and beaded headbands and bracelets.
They were taller than Connor and looked almost like sisters, except that their applied hair colors were different, blond in one
case, auburn in the other. I thought at first they would be in
some kind of competition for him which they would not disgrace themselves to acknowledge. But it was not like that at all.

In the spirit of the times they shared him, and he was dutifully shareable and slept with each of them in turn as one would imagine to be the case in any polygamous and diurnally observant household. All of that was audibly apparent after I retired as I lay in my bed upstairs and heard them going at it in the basement room where they had chosen to bunk themselves.

Where any of them came from, who their families were, I never found out, except that Lissy did tell me she grew up in San Francisco. I pictured all of them from their voices and their footsteps—and perhaps even from the volume of air they displaced. The brightest of them was Lissy. She was usually the one who thought up the things for them to do from what she found by rummaging through the house. She came up with the dressmaker's dummy lying under some other things in the drawing room and for a half day the three girls were dress designers, cutting and refitting some of our mother's old evening dresses from the closet of her room. I didn't mind. Lissy was a petite thing with short curly hair whose own frock went down to her ankles. She had made it herself, she told me in her sweetly cracked voice, it was tie-dyed in patterns of yellow and red and pink. Do you know what the color is when I mention it? she asked me. I assured her I did.

All told they would be living with us for a good month, these hippies. They were in and out of the house in no discernible pattern. They would go off to some rock-and-roll band concert and be gone for a couple of days. They would take menial jobs, make a few dollars, quit till their money ran out, and then find some other job. But for one stretch some astrological influence held sway, for they all went off to work in the morning—Lissy, a clerk in a bookshop, and Dawn and Sundown waitressing in a diner, the boys as phone solicitors for an insurance agency—and came home in the evening, just as if we were a typically square bourgeois household. That peculiar conjunction of the stars lasted almost a week.

I gathered, with the occasional overnight stays of more like them, that the word having gone out, we were part of a network of hostel-like places or pads where people could lay their heads for a night. But I was sure ours was the only pad on upper Fifth Avenue, which gave us some distinction.

Living as they did, these kids were more radical critics of society than the antiwar or civil rights people getting so much attention in the newspapers. They had no intention of trying to make things better. They had simply rejected the entire culture. If they attended that antiwar rally in the park it was because there was music there and it was pleasant to sit on the grass and drink wine and smoke their joints. They were itinerants who had chosen poverty and were too young and heedless to think what the society would eventually do to them by way of vengeance. Langley and I could have told them. They had seen our house as a Temple of Dissidence, and made it their own, so even if we had said, Look at us, look at what you might become, it wouldn't have meant anything.

In fact we were too charmed and flattered by these people to have said anything to discourage them. You would think Langley would go crazy the way they made themselves at home. They took over the kitchen at mealtimes—Dawn and Sundown would cook up great batches of vegetable stews, for of course none of them ate meat—and they slept wherever there was some space. They could at one time occupy all the bathrooms in the house, but they interested us, we attended to their diction like parents of children who were just learning to speak, and would make sure to report to each other when a word or phrase popped up that we hadn't heard before. A *put-down* was a remark to chasten or humiliate. Not to be confused with what one does to a terminally sick animal. A *turn-on* was a state of arousal—an odd electronic locution, I thought, for this vegetarian earth-loving crowd.

Fat JoJo had one day come in from his wanderings with an electric guitar and a speaker. All at once the house reverberated with awful earsplitting sounds. Fortunately I was upstairs at the time. JoJo twanged some thunderous chord and as it died out he'd sing a line from a song, and laugh, and twang another wavery chord and sing another line, and laugh. After a while I got used to JoJo's guitar—he knew he was no musician, it was a game he played, a fancy that he made fun of even as he gave himself to it. He handed it to me one day, this guitar. The strings were more like cables and they were stretched of a solid piece of wood shaped like a car with fins. I would not have thought to call it a musical instrument. Its sound made me think of those old-time vaudevillians who played a saw by bending it this way and that and running a violin bow across it.

One of JoJo's badly sung songs intrigued me. It began "Good morning, teaspoon." Langley and I discussed this. He thought that it spoke of the loneliness of the speaker ironically addressing his breakfast tableware. I disagreed. I said it was simply the speaker addressing a presumably diminutive lover waking with him in the morning, *teaspoon* being a term of endearment.

BY THIS TIME I had achieved an affection for little Lissy. Whenever she disappeared for a day or two I found myself waiting for her return. Of all of them she was the most talkative, the most fetching certainly, and the fact that I was sightless intrigued her, whereas the others merely deferred to me. One morning she found me in the kitchen by bumping into me, because she had decided to keep her eyes closed from the moment she woke up. It's not so bad, is it, she said. Oh I know I can open my eyes at any time where you can't, but right now you can see better than me, can't you? I said I could because my other faculties were a kind of recompense. And while we had this conversation I put a glass of orange juice in her hand, and she gasped.

Lissy's experiments in sightlessness brought us closer. She would feel my features, touching my forehead, nose, my mouth with her small hands, at the same time I ran my fingers over her face. She was so charming, her eyes closed, and her head averted in the manner of someone thinking of the image her hands created. Supposing this is what people did instead of kissing, I said to her. Like we were some isolated island people apart from the rest of the world. And at that I felt her lips on mine. She was standing on tiptoe to reach me and I held her waist and ran my hands down her back and felt her flesh under the thin shift she wore.

I won't pretend I was instantly and passionately in love with young Lissy. Yes, it was as if my age fell from me, but there was always in my mind an awareness of transgression—as if I was taking advantage not of this girl's generosity, but of the culture she had come out of, because she was not at all virginal, she was clearly experienced and quite comfortable climbing all over me, like some cat looking for a place to nestle down.

It doesn't make any sense at this point to gloss over things. I quote from one of our poets: "Why not say what happened?" If anyone ever reads this and thinks poorly of me—Jacqueline, if you read this you will understand, I know—but if anyone else is put out, what is that to me? I am headed in any event to a superseding namelessness.

THE ONLY SUSPENSE for me was in how much of Lissy's prattle I had to listen to on the way to the inevitable. She believed that trees were sentient. She thought people could find the answers to their problems or even know their fate by consulting a Chinese book of wisdom that she carried in her rucksack. You threw some sticks down and their arrangement told you what page to turn to. But it's just the same for you, Homer, if you open the book to any page and point your finger, she said. So I did that and she read the passage I had pointed to: Jesus, she said, I'm sorry Homer, there's "trouble ahead." Nothing I didn't know, I told her. And then she read to me from a novel in which a Buddha-inflamed German wandered about seeking enlightenment. I didn't tell her how funny I thought that was. Lissy was herself a Buddhist only insofar as she had a romantic wistful admiration for anyone who was. It was more a generalized susceptibility she had to anything Eastern. I was entranced by her sweetly cracked voice. You could almost see the little packets of sound trooping along her vocal cords one after another, some of the squeaking kind, others tumbling into the alto range.

She took it upon herself to wash my feet before I retired, saying it was an ancient custom of the desert peoples of the Near East—Jews, Christians, or Whoever. She wanted to do this and so I let her, though it was embarrassing to me. I knew my feet were far from my best feature, and having always found it difficult to trim my toenails, an arduous process, and sometimes painful, I had done that less frequently than I should have. But this Lissy didn't seem to care, she had found one of Grandmamma Robileaux's steel mixing bowls and filled it with warm water, and lay a hand towel in the water and then over my feet, and then under, lifting each foot by the heel, and washing the soles, and I had to admit it was not unpleasant. It was clearly a ceremonial washing rather than anything of practical use. These youngsters had various ceremonies of their eclectic taste, the ceremony of smoking, of drinking, of listening to music, of having sex. Their lives were one ceremony after another, and to a person who had drifted through time lacking any capacity to step out of its stream, I was prepared to learn this art with which they seemed to have been born.

One evening after washing my feet she stayed in the room with me. Her suggestion that we meditate together is what led us to lovemaking. There was really no right place to sit in the lotus position in this house. No alcove that wasn't piled high with things. My bedroom—really not even my bedroom in which the inevitable stacks of newspapers and piles of books and bric-a-brac lay about, leaving the narrowest of aisles, but my bed, a double bed which I had managed to keep sacrosanct, was the only proper platform for thinking about nothing. For that was what we were supposed to do, according to Lissy. I can't think about nothing, I said to her. The best I can do is think about myself thinking. Shhh, Homer, she said. Shhh. And when she whispered my name, God help me, the love broke over me like the hot tears of a soul that has found salvation.

Holding her arms straight up so I could lift her dress away, she emerged from her chrysalis, this tremulant wisp of a girl. Her narrow shoulders, nipples like seeds on her thin chest. And the long waist, and a pear-shaped little backside in my palms. Giving her small gift to the world, Lissy, with her childlike faith in ideas mysterious to her. Leading me through it.

Afterward, I held her in my arms and then there was a moment of mental confusion, some weird misstep of time itself, because I was briefly under the illusion that it was Sister Mary Elizabeth Riordan I was holding.

I DON'T KNOW WHY I couldn't simply enjoy the blessing of this charmingly loopy creature, the experience of her, so unsummoned, and let it go at that. Instead, I decided to torture myself by thinking about that momentary illusion while in her arms of having had my piano student. I needed to talk to Langley about it. I thought I had purged myself of any lingering feelings for Mary Elizabeth Riordan—after all she was transmogrified, a certified fifty-year-old sister. So I had debased two dear souls simultaneously, violating one in spirit and using the other for the purpose. It was no consolation to me that Lissy didn't seem to feel that anything of consequence had occurred between us. She was, at her age, in the exploratory mode characteristic of her culture. But I was deep in the doldrums now, for of course I had mostly debased myself. I knew Langley too had at that long ago time fallen in love with our piano student. I wanted to know his thinking. We had never talked about things of this sort. I was in a confessional mood. Did anybody know what love was? Could unconsummated love exist without carnal fantasy, could it survive as love without recompense, without reward? No question that I had enjoyed Lissy's giving of her body. So what did anybody love other than the genus, where one adorable creature could stand in for another?

But there didn't seem to be a right time to have this conversation with my brother. Too much was going on. As I've said, besides the original group we'd met in the park, friends of theirs, fellow squatters, had been in and out, and there were instances when I tripped over someone of whose presence I had not been aware. Or I'd hear laughter or chattering in another room and feel myself to be a guest in somebody else's house. Langley had surprised me by welcoming these people and acting toward them with uncharacteristic generosity. And they responded, taking up his daily way of life, acolytes in his Ministry. Even the thick-lensed cartoonist, Connor, liked to bring back from the street something he thought Langley would want. They all seemed to understand his acquisitiveness as an ethos. I was fairly sure that he wasn't involved with any of the girls— running these people seemed to be how he was relating to them, they could have been kid pickpockets in London and he Fagin. The only audience he'd had in all these years was me. Now he was an adopted guru. How they cheered when he kicked the water-meter reader out of the basement!

At times things got noisy as something clanging would be brought in through the front door. Langley himself had discovered the neighborhood down at the Bowery where secondhand restaurant supplies were out on the sidewalk, and so to end our indebtedness to the gas company he bought a portable, two-burner kerosene stove, thus retiring the massive old eight-burner gas stove on which Grandmamma Robileaux had done her cooking. Langley would risk death by asphyxiation to defeat the gas company. Also sets of crockery and dishes, bowls, and implements like spatulas—this was to give our guests whatever they needed to prepare our community meals. And that electric guitar of JoJo's had inspired further acquisitions—speakers, microphones, and recording consoles, Langley saying to me, knowing I was not the biggest fan of the electronic sound, that these were things we could rent out, the number of aspiring musicians who wanted to play electric guitars increasing exponentially day by day, as he could tell by reading the entertainment sections of the newspapers. It's no more Swing and Sway with Sammy Kaye, he told me. No more Horace Heidt and His Musical Knights. It's electrified musicians who give themselves existential names and command huge audiences of slightly younger people who want themselves to go out and pump their pelvis and scream and twang their earsplitting music to stadiums full of idiots.

So as I say, somehow I could never find the opportunity to sit Langley down and have him consider my despondent contribution to his Theory of Replacements. He assumed the passage of generations, you see, but my idea was lateral. If what mattered was the universal form of Dear Girl, and if each dear girl was only a particular expression of the universal, any one of them might serve equally well, and could replace another as our morally insufficient nature demanded. And if that were the case how could I ever be educated to love anyone for a lifetime?

Lissy, I reiterate, did in no way suffer my duplicity. She asked no questions, was quite incurious about my past life except for the novelty of my sightlessness. We did make love another time or two and then it became apparent to me that my bed, one of the more desirable accommodations in our house, was of more interest to her as a place to sleep. For a while we continued to meditate or, as I understood it, to sit quietly together, and she one day brought in from her wanderings some homeopathic remedies in anticipation of the coming flu season, she said, and pressed these vials into my hands and kissed me on the cheek. We were friends and if she had slept with me, well, that's what friends did.

—

AND IT WAS GETTING colder now, was it November by this time? I don't recall. But none of these people could accept winter. For one thing they hadn't the stamina for it, their marginal existence demanded a beneficent climate, some steady changeless warmth in which they could survive with the least effort. They availed themselves of some of the army issue still lying around—Lissy's found field jacket coming to her knees—so I knew they would soon, like any other flock of migratory birds, lift their wings and be off.

I assumed it was in anticipation of their departure that they prepared a big dinner for us all to have at the same time. For some reason the front hall was less filled with things than any of the rooms, and so our hippies dug up our candelabra, and candlesticks, and availed themselves of our supply of candles, of which we had many and of different kinds, including candle wax in glass tumblers that Langley had found in a shop down on the Lower East Side, and these were put on the floor in a manner to suggest a dining table, and cushions gathered from all over the house were placed about for our bottoms, and so Langley and I were invited to seat ourselves, which we did laboriously in the cross-legged position, like pashas, while our boarders trooped in with the food and wine. Apparently all of them had worked at this, each contributing a specialty, sautéed mushrooms, bowls of salad and vegetable soup, fondue with toasted points of bread, and steamed artichokes, and oysters, and clams boiled in beer—I assumed that was JoJo's contribution—and hard cheese and red table wine, and pastries and marijuana cigarettes for dessert. They had paid for everything and it was all by way of thanks, and it was very moving. Langley and I for the first and last time in our lives smoked joints, and my memory of the rest of the evening is a little blurry, except that both Dawn and Sundown seemed to have discovered me at this late date, and they came over and sat beside me and gave me hugs and we all laughed together, finding it funny for some reason as I pressed their ample bosoms to my chest and nuzzled their necks. Toasts were given, and if I'm not mistaken a solemn moment of remembrance for the three great men who'd been assassinated in the course of a decade. I like to think, too, that Lissy may have moved to repossess me for herself during the course of the evening for it was she who led me up to my room afterward, navigating the stairs for me—I was thoroughly stoned, they had moved on from the marijuana to hash, a somewhat more potent drug—and she lay down beside me on my bed, where I had a vision: it was of sailing ships and they were as if etched on a salver of pewter. I said, Lissy, do you see the ships? And she touched her temple to mine and at that moment the ships were as if hammered on a sheet of gold, and she said, Oh wow, they're so beautiful, oh wow.

I do remember these moments so clearly, my mind as out of control as it was. I have never since taken, or done, any such drugs, not wanting to tamper with what consciousness I have. But it's undeniable that those moments had their uncanny clarity. I must have dozed off but came awake to find Lissy holding me, and my shirt wet from her tears. I asked her why she was crying but she wouldn't answer, only shaking her head. Was it because I was an old man and she was overwhelmed with pity? Had she realized, finally, the ruinous state of this house? I didn't know what it was about—and concluded it was nothing more than the emotional overload of a stoned mind. I held her and we fell asleep that way.

BUT A FEW MORE DAYS were to pass before the exodus. I was at my piano—this was in the evening, I believe I was doing the elegiac slow movement of Mozart's Twentieth—when other sounds began to intrude and these gradually defined themselves as shouts, and they were coming from all over the house. Apparently the lights had gone out. I at first thought Langley had blown something—one of his most sacred long-term missions being to defeat the Consolidated Edison Company—but in fact it was the whole city's power failure, and it was as if a time of pre-civilization had come around again to deliver the meaning of night. Oddly enough, once people looked out the window and understood the extent of the blackout, everyone wanted to see it—all our squatters clamoring to get out there and be amazed by the moonlit city. I considered the possibility that this municipal blown fuse was, after all, something for which Langley's tinkering was responsible, and it made me laugh. Langley! I called to him. What have you done!

He was upstairs in his room and was having as much trouble as the rest of them trying to get to the front door. It was the blind brother who got everyone organized, telling them not to move, but to stay where they were until I came and got them. Nobody could have found a candle—where any candles or candle glasses were nobody knew by now, the chances of finding even one in the blackness of the house was nil, the candles had consigned themselves to our kingdom of rubble as had everything else.

The house by this time of our lives was a labyrinth of hazardous pathways, full of obstructions and many dead ends. With enough light someone could make his way through the zigzagging corridors of newspaper bales, or find passage by slipping sideways between piles of equipment of one kind or another— the guts of pianos, motors wrapped in their power cords, boxes of tools, paintings, car body parts, tires, stacked chairs, tables on tables, headboards, barrels, collapsed stacks of books, antique lamps, dislodged pieces of our parents' furniture, rolled-up carpet, piles of clothing, bicycles—but it needed the native gifts of a blind man who sensed where things were by the air they displaced to get from one room to another without killing himself in the process. As it was, I tripped several times, and fell down once and hurt my elbow, in the meantime finding people from the top of the house down, as I asked them to call out, one by one, and telling them to attach themselves to me, like boxcars to an engine. And it turned out to be a good time I was having actually as the deviser of this human train that wound its way through the Collyer residence, everyone laughing or yelping in pain as they banged their knees or tripped. And the train got heavier to pull along with each new person who hooked on—

clearly there were more of our hippie friends in residence than I had known about. Of course Lissy was the first one I had managed to find and I felt her hands on my waist as she giggled. This is so cool! she said. Then she decided we all had the makings of a conga line—how she had known about a dance that went out of fashion before she was ever born, I don't know. But there she was, trying to instruct me and everyone behind her in that hip-shifting one-two-three followed by the leg-out BAM! which of course created even more chaos as the others tried to do it. I heard Langley at the very end of the line, and he was having a good time too, it was remarkable hearing my brother's wheezing laugh, truly remarkable. And it was the darkness that made all of this possible—their darkness, not mine—and when I reached the front hall and lifted off the two-by-four dead bolt and opened the door, they all flew past me like birds from the cage, and I think it was Lissy's kiss I felt on my cheek, though it may have been Dawn or Sundown's, and I felt the brisk night air and stood at the top of the stoop and inhaled the earthy fragrance of the park, edged with the metallic taste of moonlight, and I heard their laughter as they fled across the street and into the park, all of them, including my brother, though he would come back, but the others, never, their laughter diminishing through the trees, for that was the last of them, they were gone.

OF COURSE I MISSED them, I missed their appreciation of us, if that is the word. I envied their unsafe lives. Whether their vagrancy was the heedlessness of youth or had at its basis some principled if inarticulate dissent was hard to know. It was a cultural wave that had lifted them, certainly, the war in Vietnam could not completely account for it, and any one of them might have had no more initiative than to be swept up into the wave. Still, in this house, now so terribly quiet, I felt my true age reclaiming me. Having all those people around had led me to understand that our habitual reclusion was needful. When they were gone and once again it was just my brother and me, my spirits slumped. We were our bothered selves once again with the world outside contesting with us as if it had withdrawn its ambassadors.

OUR TROUBLES BEGAN with that kerosene stove Langley had brought in. It caught fire one morning as he was cooking our omelets. I was sitting at the kitchen table and I heard this small pufflike explosion. Of course we had accumulated several fire extinguishers of different kinds and makes over the years, but whichever of them was in the kitchen was of small use—I suppose their potency evaporates over time. He gave me a running account of what was happening in a voice of controlled urgency, Langley—that the foam from the extinguisher was just enough to leave the stove temporarily fireless but smoking. I could smell it. He wrapped it in dish towels and threw the whole thing out the kitchen door into the backyard.

That seemed to have solved the problem. I knew my brother was embarrassed by the quiet way he closed the kitchen door, and I said nothing as we ate a cold breakfast.

It wasn't more than an hour later when I heard sirens. I was at the Aeolian and thinking nothing about it—you heard fire engines and ambulances day and night in this city. I found the siren's notes on the piano—A's sliding into B-flats and back to A's—but then the sound got closer and died into a low growl seemingly right in front of the house. Poundings on the door, shouts of Where is it, where is it? as this herd of firemen clambered in, pushing me aside, cursing as they tried to find their way to the kitchen, and dragging hose behind them, which I tripped over, Langley shouting What are you doing in this house, get out get out! They had been called by the people in the brownstone next door, whose garden abutted our backyard. In all these years we'd never met these neighbors or spoken to them, we didn't know who they were except as the likely culprits who'd left an unsigned letter in our mail protesting our tea dances of so many years before. And now they had reported that our backyard was on fire, which happened to have been the case. Why can't these people ever mind their own business, Langley muttered as the fire hose, connected now to the hydrant at the curb in front of the house, pulsed through the labyrinth of baled newspapers and slapped this way and that into folded chairs and bridge tables, knocking down standing lamps, stacks of canvases, as the firemen aimed their nozzle through the back door down to the smoking racks of lumber, the used tires, and odd pieces of furniture, a legless bureau, a bedspring, two Adirondack chairs, and other items stored there in the expectation that someday we would find use for them.

Langley would insist afterward that the firemen had overre-
acted, though the smell of smoke would linger for weeks. When
an inspector from the Fire Department arrived he looked over
the smoking rubble and said we would be issued a summons
and most likely fined for illegal storing of flammable materials
in a residential neighborhood. Langley said if that were the case
we would sue the Fire Department for the destruction of property. Your men's boots have left a trail of mud on our floors, he
said, the back door of the kitchen is off its hinges, they have
stormed through here like vandals as you can see from these
broken vases, these lamps here, and look at these valuable books
soggy and bloated from the damn leaks in their hose.

Well, Mr. Collyer, is it? I should think it's a small price to
pay for having still an abode to live in.

The fire inspector, whom I took for an intelligent man of
some years—he had used the word *abode*, a word you did not
often hear in ordinary conversation—surely had looked around,
taking it all in, and though he didn't say anything, he must have
passed on what he had seen of our rooms for within a week or
so we received a certified letter from the Health Department
requesting an appointment for the purpose of assessing the interior condition of—and here they indicated our home by its
address.

We of course ignored the letter but our sense of a diminished
freedom was palpable. All it took was for people with official
credentials to have intentions regarding us. I think it was at this
time that Langley ordered a complete course of law books from

some college in the Midwest that offered a law degree by mail. By the time the books arrived—in a crate—we were in the sights not only of the Health Department, but of a collection agency acting on behalf of the New York Telephone Company, of lawyers from Consolidated Edison for having damaged their property—I assume they meant the electric meter in the basement, an irritating buzzing thingamajig which we had silenced with a hammer—and of the Dime Savings Bank, which had inherited our mortgage and claimed that in failing to meet our payments we were facing foreclosure, and the Woodlawn Cemetery had drawn a bead because we had somehow forgotten to pay the bills for the care of our parents' grave site. That wasn't all of it—there were other letters popping through the mail slot in the front door whose contents I can't recall just now. But for some reason it was the cemetery bill that most engaged my brother's attention. Homer, he said, can you think of anyone as depraved as these people who live on death even to the point of charging good money for snipping some leaves of grass around a headstone? After all who cares what graves look like? Certainly not their occupants. What a fraud, this is sheer irreverence, the professional care of the dead. Let the whole cemetery go back to its wild state I say. Just as it was in the days of the Manhattan Indians—let there be a necropolis of tilted stones and fallen angels lying half hidden in the North American forest. And that to me would show true respect for the dead, that would be a sacred acknowledgment, in beauty, of the awful system of life and death.

—

I HAD THE IDEA of ranking our problems as a means of solving them and the mortgage seemed to me the first order of business. It was a struggle to get Langley to sit down and go over our finances. He felt attention to these matters rendered one subservient. But I realized from his reading of the account books that we had sufficient funds to pay off the mortgage altogether. Let's do that and get these people off our backs, I said, and never again will we have to worry about it.

We lose the deduction on our federal taxes if we pay off the damn thing, Langley said.

But we're not getting the deduction if we're not meeting the payments, I told him. All we're getting is penalties that offset the deduction. And why are we talking about taxes since we don't pay them.

He had an answer for that having to do with the war, though it went on from there and I'm not sure I can render it accurately. Something about primitive societies that function brilliantly without money, and then a discourse on corporate usury, and then he burst into song: "Oh the banks are made of marble / With a guard at every door / And the vaults are stuffed with silver / That the miner sweated for." Langley's tone-deaf, hoarse baritone was an instrument of undeniable power. I did not laugh or speak of the genetic caprices in life whereby a musical gift could be designated in its entirety to one brother, namely me. I did wonder what miners had to do with anything. Homer, he said, I remind you of the derivation of our name. Were not our paternal ancestors diggers in the bowels of the earth? Were they not coal miners? Is a collier not a coal miner?

Soon we were discussing other trade names—Baker, Cooper, Farmer, Miller—and mulling over of the turnings of history in such names, and that was the end of our financial conference.

Langley would eventually agree with me and pay off the mortgage but by that time we were famous throughout the city and he was followed to the bank by newspaper reporters, and a photographer for the *Daily News,* who would win a Pulitzer Prize for his portrait of Langley shuffling down Fifth Avenue in a porkpie hat, a ragged coat down to his ankles, a shawl he'd made from a burlap sack, and house slippers.

I WILL SAY IN MY brother's defense that he had a lot on his mind. It was a period of appalling human behavior—for instance the bombing of the Baptist church down south in which four little black girls were killed while at Sunday school. The news left him distraught—there were occasions, you see, when his cynicism broke down and the heart was made visible. But the monstrousness of what had happened revealed to him yet another category of seminal events for his ultimate newspaper—the murder of innocents, not only for those little girls, but for the shooting down of college students, and for the slaying of young men registering people to vote, in that same appalling period. And then of course he had to open a file for political assassinations—we had had three or four of those—and perhaps a file for the mass detention of hundreds of street demonstrators in an outside pen in Washington. He couldn't decide if that event should be incorporated into the category of club-on-the-head police conduct as applied to antiwar demonstrators in other cities, or whether it was something different.

Langley's dream newspaper could not be mere reportage, its single edition for all time demanded a painfully categorical account of what we are given to habitually as a specie. So it was a big organizational problem for him to cull from years of daily newspapers the signal episodes and kinds of activities that are timeless.

He would be tested in the years following: he told me one day about the mass suicide of nine hundred people living in a small South American country I had never heard of before. They were Americans who had fled there to live in rows of shacks which their leader proposed to them as an idealistic Communist paradise. They had practiced suicide by drinking a harmless red liquid in lieu of poison, but when it came time that their leader said they could no longer tolerate the repression of the outside world, they did not hesitate to swallow the real thing. All nine hundred of them. I asked Langley, Where do you put this event? He said he thought at first to file it under Fashion, as when everybody is all at once wearing the new color. Or when the same slang word is suddenly on everybody's lips. But finally, he said, I've put it in a pending file of one-of-a-kind headline events. There it must stay awaiting another episode of insane lemminglike behavior to pop up again. As I suspect it will, he added.

Presidential malfeasance in these years was another entry for his conditional file. Until another president subverted the Constitution he was sworn to uphold, it couldn't be considered as seminal. But I'm waiting, he said.

ONE DAY MY BROTHER came in with his morning papers and without saying a word he went to the windows and began pulling the shutters together and locking them. I heard the banging of the shutters slamming in place like heavy doors and watched the patina of lighter darkness receding from my eyes. The house air became cooler. A strange strangled sound came from my brother's throat that I only slowly realized was his effort not to break down.

An awful feeling, a constriction of the heart, caused me to rise from my piano bench. What is it? I said.

He read to me: The bodies of four American nuns in a remote Central American village had been found in shallow graves. They had been raped and shot to death. Their names had not yet been released.

I didn't want to believe what I knew. I insisted that without the names we couldn't be sure that Mary Elizabeth Riordan was one of the nuns.

Langley climbed upstairs and found the little tin box where we kept her letters. She had written us from time to time as her order moved her about the world: she had gone from one African country to another, and then to South Asian countries and, after some years, to villages in Central America. The letters were always the same wherever she was, as if she was on a world tour of destitution and death. Dear friends, she had written in her last letter, I am here in this bereft little country torn by civil war. Just last week soldiers came through and took away several men of the village and killed them for being with the insurgency. They were only poor farmers trying to feed their families. It is only old men, women, and children now. They cry out in their sleep. Three of my sisters are here with me. We provide what solace we can.

The letter had been written a few months before from the same village named in the newspaper.

I AM NOT A religious person. I prayed to be forgiven for having been jealous of her calling, for having longed for her, for having despoiled her in my dreams. But in truth I have to admit that I was numbed enough by this awful fate of the sister to be not quite able to connect it with my piano student Mary Elizabeth Riordan. Even now, I have the clean scent of her as we sit together on the piano bench. I can summon that up at will. She speaks softly in my ear as, night after night, the moving pictures roll by: Here it's a funny chase with people hanging out of cars . . . here the hero is riding a horse at a gallop . . . here firemen are sliding down a pole . . . and here (I feel her hand on my shoulder) the lovers embrace, they're looking into each other's eyes, and now the card says . . . "I love you."

—

AFTER SOME DAYS of silence in our house I said to Langley: This is martyrdom, this is what martyrdom is.

Why, said Langley, because they were nuns? Martyrdom is a religious invention. If it isn't, why do you not say the four little girls murdered in their Sunday school in Birmingham are martyrs?

I thought about this. I could see the possibility that the sister would have forgiven her abuser and touched his face with two fingers as he brought his gun up to her temple.

There is a difference, I said. The nuns' religious beliefs put them in harm's way. They knew there was a civil war, that armed savages roamed the land.

You idiot! Langley shouted. Who do you think armed them! They're our savages!

But now I am not sure when all of this happened. Either my mind is turning in on itself and its memories are eliding, or I have finally understood the prophecy of Langley's timeless newspaper.

OUR SHUTTERS WERE never again to be opened. Langley made arrangements with the newsstand where he got his papers to have them delivered to our front door. The early editions of the morning papers arrived usually at about eleven at night. The evening papers were left at our door by three in the afternoon.

When Langley did go out, it was always at night. He did our marketing at a small grocery store that had opened just a few blocks north of us and that sold day-old bread. He made a point of patronizing this store, of buying more than we needed, actually, because a local free newspaper that covered embassy receptions, and fashion shows, and ran interviews with interior decorators reported that the store owner was Hispanic. My heavens, Langley shouted, run for your lives, they're here!

In truth that was one sign of a changing city—a slow, almost imperceptible lapping of a tide from the north—but something like a little grocery store, or a couple of Negro faces seen on the street, was enough for our neighbors to throw up their hands. And, of course, inevitably, my brother and I were deemed the First Cause—it was the Collyers, to the manner born, who had fomented this disaster. Whatever animosity had been directed at us since the fire in our backyard—no: that had been building since the time of our tea dances—was now in full cry.

Fairly regularly we received unsigned letters of vilification. I remember a day when the envelopes slid through the mail slot and fell on the floor in a way to make me think of fish flopping out of a net. We were threatened, we were cursed, and one day an envelope we opened had for its message a dead cockroach. Was that a little hieroglyph to represent us in the view of the correspondent? Or did that mean we were held responsible for infesting the neighborhood with vermin? It is true that we had cockroaches—had had them for as long as I could remember. They never bothered me, I would feel something crawling on my ankle and brush it away as I would a fly or a mosquito.

Langley respected cockroaches as having a kind of intelligence, or even personality, with their cunning evasiveness, and their bravery, as when under attack they would leap off a counter into the unknown. And they could indicate their displeasure with a hiss or a squeak. Nevertheless we did have traps set out for them and of course it was nonsense to blame us for the infestation of other houses. People in this neighborhood were embarrassed to admit their own distinguished homes were pest-ridden. But cockroaches had been city residents since the days of Peter Stuyvesant.

Langley had set aside his newspapers, stacking the dailies for future reading, because his legal studies with the mail-order law school now took most of his time. This was not a mere academic exercise. He was attempting to hold off not only the utilities and other creditors, but also the Health and Fire Departments, both of whom were demanding entry, in order to find things to alarm them. He was able to find a city statute that complicated things for them when they threatened to get court orders. He had also gone out and secured a Legal Aid Society lawyer, who, for no fee, was prepared at Langley's instruction to make various legal motions, as impediments, when and if things progressed to the next stage, as we assumed they would. Overall we would take the position that a mere cursory examination by that Fire Department inspector after the backyard fire—which is what had set off all this hullabaloo—was not sufficient cause to violate the constitutional sanctity of a man's home.

It was clear to me that Langley relished all this, and I was glad to see that he was engaged in a practical enterprise for a change. It brought a here-and-now component to his life, an immediacy, and the promise, good or bad, of an outcome, which was not the case with his eternal, never-to-be-achieved, Platonic newspaper. My only contribution was to listen every now and then to an example he had found of legal reasoning that seemed to him to have come out of an insane asylum.

It certainly didn't help us in our relations with the neighbors and contretemps with the city bureaucracies that all of New York at this time was experiencing a deterioration in the civil order: municipal services breaking down—uncollected garbage, graffitied subway cars—street crimes rising, drug addicts abounding. I understood too that our professional sports teams were doing badly in the standings.

Under these circumstances, our closed shutters and the two-by-four bolt on our front door seemed to make sense. My life now was entirely in the house.

IT WAS AROUND this time that I noticed my precious Aeolian was off by a half tone in the middle octaves. The bass notes and the treble notes seemed all right, and this is what I found strange, that the piano would have gone out of tune in that discretionary manner. I thought, well of course, since the shutters had been closed, the house had become noticeably musty, and with everything gathering dust in every room, everything you could imagine piled almost to the ceiling, as well as the newspaper bales that served as walls for our mazelike pathways, it was no wonder that a delicate instrument would be affected. On a rainy day the dampness was palpable and the odor of the basement mildew seemed to come up through the floor.

There were other pianos of course, or piano innards. Some were definitely out of tune in the usual way, as why would they not be—but I began to be alarmed when I turned on the player piano, which I had kept covered with a plastic sheet, and heard that same sharpness in the middle octaves. Then I groped around till I found the little portable electric piano, a computer actually—with different settings it would sound like a flute or a violin or an accordion, and so on—that Langley had recently brought into the house. I remember being grateful that it could sit comfortably on a table. Because Langley's first computer was the size of a refrigerator, a huge bulky thing with vacuum tubes that he had been able to buy—for a song, he said—only because it was an obsolete model. He was not able to put it to the test and see if it did whatever computers did—something in the nature of calculations, he said, and when I asked calculations of what, he said of anything—because by the time he would figure out what to do with it we would have no electricity. So I didn't understand how this little computer that looked like a keyboard and that worked on batteries did whatever calculations it had to do to play music, except that it did. And when I flicked on the switch, and played a scale, this instrument, with nothing like strings to go out of tune, was out of tune in the middle register, just like my Aeolian.

At that moment I understood it was not any piano but my hearing that was off-key. I was hearing a C as a C-sharp. That was the beginning. I shrugged and persuaded myself that I could live with it. The pieces in my repertoire I could hear by memory as if nothing was wrong. But over time it would become not just a matter of pitch, of an off-key sound, but of no sound at all. I didn't want to believe that was happening even as I understood that it was, slowly but surely. Months were to go by before, decibel by decibel, the world would grow muffled and I would lose my prideful hearing entirely and so be worse off than Beethoven, who could at least see.

If it had happened all of a sudden that I was to lose the last sense that connected me to the world, I would have screamed in terror and found some way as quickly as possible to end my life. But it came upon me gradually, allowing me progressive degrees of acceptance, with hope that every degree of loss would be the last, until, in the growing quiet of my despair, I resolved to accept my fate, having been taken by an odd impulse to find out what life would be like when my hearing was completely gone and, without sight or sound, I had only my own consciousness to amuse me.

I did not tell Langley about any of this. I don't know why. Perhaps I thought that he would instantly add ears to his medical practice. It had reached the point where for the recovery of my eyesight he had prescribed for breakfast every morning seven peeled oranges and with lunch two eight-ounce glasses of orange juice and with dinner an orange cordial instead of my preferred glass of Almaden wine. If I had told him my hearing was awry he would have surely found some Langleyan cure for that. Under the circumstances I kept my own counsel and distracted myself with the problems we were having with the outside world.

I'M NOT SURE WHEN our battles with the Health and Fire Departments, the bank, the utilities, and everyone else who was demanding some kind of satisfaction attracted the notice of the press. I will not pretend to a precision of remembrance as I try to tell of our life in this house in these last few years. Time seems to me a drift, a shifting of sand. And my mind is shifting with it. I am wearing away. I feel I have not the leisure to tax myself for the right date, the right word. The best I can do is put things down as they occur to me and hope for the best. Which is a shame for as I've kept to this task I've developed a taste for an exact rendering of our lives, seeing and hearing with words if with nothing else.

The first reporter who rang our bell—a really stupid young man who expected to be invited in, and when we wouldn't permit that, stood there asking offensive questions, even shouting them out after we had slammed the door—made me realize it was a class of disgustingly fallible human beings who turned themselves into infallible print every day, compounding the historical record that stood in our house like bales of cotton. If you talk to these people you are at their mercy, and if you don't talk to them you are at their mercy. Langley said to me, We are a story, Homer. Listen to this—and he read this supposedly factual account about these weird eccentrics who had shuttered their windows and bolted their doors and run up thousands of dollars in unpaid bills though they were worth millions. It had our ages wrong, Langley was called Larry, and a neighbor, unnamed, thought we kept women against their will. That our house was a blight on the neighborhood was never in question. Even the abandoned peregrine nest up under the roof ledge was held against us.

I said to my brother: How would you run this in Collyer's forever up-to-date newspaper?

We are sui generis, Homer, he said. Unless someone comes along as remarkably prophetic as we are, I'm obliged to ignore our existence.

THE ATTENTION FROM the press was not continuous, but we had become a stop on the beat, as it were, a reliable source of wonder for the reading public. We could laugh about this, at least at the beginning, but it became less funny and more alarming as time went on. Some of these reporters published the details of our parents' lives—when they bought the house and how much they paid for it—all matters of public record if you had nothing better to do than go downtown and dig through city archives. And they found out from old census reports and ship manifests when our ancestors arrived on these shores—it was early in the nineteenth century—and where they lived, their generations, artisans risen to the professions, the marriages made, the children begotten, and so forth. So now all of that was public knowledge but what was the point except to indicate the decline of a House, the Fall of a reputable family, the shame of all that history in that it had led to us, the without-issue Collyer brothers lurking behind closed doors and coming out only at night.

I admit to feeling at secret times, usually just before falling asleep, that if one held to conventional bourgeois values he could read the Collyer brothers as end-of-the-line. Then I would get angry with myself. After all, we were living original self-directed lives unintimidated by convention—could we not be a supreming of the line, a flowering of the family tree?

Langley said: Who cares who our distinguished ancestors were? What balderdash. All those census records, all those archives, attest only to the self-importance of the human being who gives himself a name and a pat on the back and doesn't admit how irrelevant he is to the turnings of the planet.

I wasn't prepared to go that far, for if you felt that way what was the use of living in the world, of believing in yourself as an identifiable person with an intellect and desires and the ability to learn and to affect outcomes? But of course Langley liked to say these things, he had been saying them all our adult lives, and for someone who had no regard for his own distinctiveness, he was certainly putting up a struggle, holding off the city agencies, the creditors, the neighbors, the press and relishing the battle. Oh and then one night he thought he had heard something scurrying about the house. I could hear it too when he brought it to my attention. We stood in the living room and listened. A clicking sound that I thought was above our heads. He thought it was inside the wall. Was it one creature or more than one? We couldn't tell but whatever it was, it was weirdly busy, busier than we were. Langley decided we had mice. I didn't tell him I thought it might be something larger. By this time I wouldn't have heard mice. The sound was not that of something small, and not of a timid interloper, but of something living in our house impertinently, without our leave. This was a creature with clear intentions. Listening to its busy click click click I imagined it as arranging things to its satisfaction. It was unnerving, how presumptive the sound was, almost as to make me think I was the interloper. And if it was inside the walls or between the floors, how could we hope it would stay there without venturing into the house proper?

Langley went out that night and came back with two stray cats, and set them out to catch whatever it was, and when that didn't bring immediate results he added another three or four, all of them strays—tough street cats with loud voices—until we had a half dozen roaming among our crowded rooms like sentries, cats that had to be fed and spoken to and with litter boxes that had to be emptied. My brother, who had no regard for the pretensions of the human race, turned out to have the feelings of a fond father for these feral cats. They climbed upon the jumbles or piles or stacks of things and liked to leap down onto our shoulders. I would sometimes trip over one, for they had lengthy rest periods and lay about, upstairs and down, and if I stepped on a tail and produced a hissing protest Langley would say, Homer, try to be more careful.

So now we had cats on patrol, slinking everywhere around and under everything, and I still heard the toenail clicks in the ceiling at night as I lay in bed, and sometime a scratching at the walls. But this was not an exclusively nocturnal animal—I could hear it running about in the daytime as well, particularly when I stood in the dining room. I don't think I have mentioned the elaborate crystal chandelier that hung in the dining room. Apparently the mysterious creature or family of creatures—for I was coming to believe that more than one was involved—had so befouled their residence over the dining room that the sodden ceiling buckled, looking, said Langley, like the bottom of the moon, and down came the chandelier—like some sort of parachute on a cable—shattering against the Model T, the pendant crystals flying off in every direction and scattering the yowling cats.

I remembered seeing, as a child, one of my mother's maids standing on a ladder under that chandelier and removing each crystal, cleaning it with a cloth, and hanging it back on its hook. She had let me hold one. I was surprised at how heavy it was—it was shaped like two slender pyramids with their bases stuck together and when I told her that she had smiled and said what a smart boy I was.

OUR DIFFICULTIES WITH the bank that held our mortgage—by now the Dime Savings Bank, for these things are traded about, just as the banks themselves undergo metamorphoses, the original Corn Exchange of which I was so fond having become the Chemical Corn Exchange, with maybe the seeds of a potent hybrid crop secreted within its vaults, and then the Corn disappeared, perhaps burned away by its chemical components, and lo, it was the Chase Chemical and then the chemistry was gone and it was the rock-hard Chase Manhattan, and so on, in the endless process of corporate mutations in which nothing changes or is improved, according to Langley—but anyway, our difficulties with the Dime Savings culminated in a contretemps at the top of our front steps, with an actual banker—accompanied by a city marshal to suggest what an eviction would feel like—standing there and waving a summons in my face and, presumably, Langley's as well.

We were, the four of us, standing at the top of the steps, the brothers confronting the two unwelcome guests, who, with their backs to the street, were, militarily speaking, in an indefensible position. I listened to the banker intone our dire fate—he was a baritone with a supercilious Park Avenue diction—and thought, If he breezes those papers in front of my nose one more time I shall give him a shove and listen to the fracturings of his skull as he goes down backward on our granite stoop. It was unlike me to contemplate violence—I was surprised by it myself and not entirely displeased—but Langley, from whom one would expect something that radical, said, Just wait a moment, and withdrew inside to emerge a minute later with one of his mail-order law books in hand. I heard the shuffle of the pages. Ah yes, he said, all right then, I accept your summons—give it here—and will see you at court—let's see—the hearing should be in about six to eight weeks, as I understand these matters.

All you need do to avoid foreclosure, said the banker, somewhat disconcerted—for he had not expected any legal knowledge of us and a court hearing meant lawyers for the bank and endless protraction of the dispute before any eviction could occur—all you need do, sir, is retire the months in arrears and the bank will consider our customer relationship as in the past and there will be no need for a court hearing. We have had a long and amenable relationship with the Collyer family and have no wish to have it end badly.

Langley: No that's all right. Even if a judge rules in your favor, which is not at all certain given your usurious four-point-five percent interest rate, he will issue a *lis pendens*, which as you know is a redemption period of another three months. Let's see, on top of the two months until we appear in court that's almost a half year before we have to do anything, or retire anything. And who knows, we might before the final bell decide to pay off the whole damn mortgage, or maybe not. Who can tell? Good day to you, sir. We do appreciate your taking time out of your busy banker's day to personally call on us but now, if you don't mind, take your marshal with you and get the hell off our property.

BY THE FOLLOWING spring we did pay off the mortgage. As I believe I've mentioned, Langley decided to do that in person. After having advised the bank by mail when he would appear, he walked from our house on upper Fifth Avenue to the Dime

Savings on Worth Street in the Financial District, a distance nearly half the length of Manhattan.

Typically, the press got it wrong: my brother wasn't trying merely to save carfare—that was a secondary consideration. Really he wanted to keep the officers of the Dime Savings in a state of suspense.

WITH LANGLEY ON his way that morning, I decided to get some air. I put on a clean shirt, an old but very comfortable cashmere sweater, my tweed jacket, and a reasonably unworn pair of trousers. If any reporters were hanging about I assumed that Langley would have drawn them off and I could get across to the park without incident. Also, it was fairly early in the day when the curiosity seekers were less likely to be found lingering in front of the house. That is what the newspaper stories had done for us, you see, made our home something to stare at, and there were times, usually on the weekends, when a small crowd would have gathered to look at our boarded-up windows, hoping for one of the maniac brothers to step outside and shake his fist at them. Or they would point at the gap in the cornice where the marble corbel had fallen to the sidewalk—have I mentioned that?—almost hitting someone walking past at that moment, except that it hadn't and he had to be content with a suit claiming a small chip of the marble had flown up and damaged his eye. But with all these people coming around—if two or three were standing there and a passerby wondered what was going on, he would stop as well—they would engage in conversation, some of which I could hear when I stood behind the shutter of a window that was open a crack. It amazed me how proprietary some of these people felt—you'd think it was their house falling to pieces.

But at this time everything sounded quiet enough. I walked out into a warm spring morning and stood at the curb waiting for a lull in the traffic. My hearing at this point having lost a degree of its brilliance I thought the moment had come, and I'd already stepped off the curb when a woman called out No!—or *Non!*—for this was Jacqueline Roux, the about-to-be dear friend of my end of life—even at the same time as I heard tires screech and horns blow, perhaps even fenders creasing, but in any case I stood transfixed, having stopped traffic. Through all of this, footsteps approaching, and the same confident voice behind me saying, All right, now we may go, and her arm through my arm and her hand gripping my hand as, despite the shouts and curses, we walked unhurriedly across Fifth Avenue like old friends out for a stroll. And in this way, and not the only time, did Jacqueline Roux save my life.

I AM IN THE DARKNESS and silence deeper than the poet's sea-dingle but I see that morning in the park and hear her voice and remember her words as if I was back outside of myself and the world was before me. She found us a bench in the sun, asked me my name and told me hers. I thought she must be remarkably self-assured to take charge of a blind man and then, having done the good deed, to sit down to talk with him. People who help you usually make a quick exit.

This is so perfect, she said.

A match was struck. I smelled the acrid smoke of one of her European cigarettes. I heard her inhale to get the smoke as far into herself as she could.

Because you are just the man I was coming to see, she said.

Me? You know who I am?

Oh yes, Homer Collyer, you and your brother are famous now in France.

Good God. Don't tell me you're a reporter.

Well, it's true, I write sometime for the papers.

Look, I know you've just saved my life—

Oh, poof—

—and I should really be more gracious, but the fact is my brother and I don't talk to reporters.

She didn't seem to hear me. You have a good face, she said, good features, and your eyes, even so, are rather attractive. But too thin, you are too thin, and a barber would be advisable.

She inhaled, she exhaled: I am not here to interview you. I am to write about your country. I have been everywhere because I don't know what I am looking for.

She had been to California and the Northwest, she had been to the Mojave Desert and to Chicago and Detroit, and to Appalachia, and now here she was with me on a park bench.

If I am a reporter, she said, it is to report on my own self, my own feelings for what I discover. I am trying to get this country—is that how you say it, to *get* something is to understand it? I have leave for a very impressionist Jacqueline Roux commentary for *Le Monde*—yes a newspaper, but my commentary is not to be where I've been or who I've talked to, but what I have learned of your secrets.

What secrets?

I am to write about what cannot be seen. It is difficult.

To take our measure.

All right, yes, that. When I found your address I looked at your house with its black shutters. In Europe we have shutters for the windows, not here so much I should have thought. In France, in Italy, in Germany, the shutters are because of our history. History makes it advisable to have heavy shutters on the windows, and to close them at night. In this country the homes are not hidden behind walls, within courtyards. You have not enough history for that. Your homes confront the street unafraid, for everyone to see. So why do you have black shutters on your windows, Homer Collyer? What does it mean for the Collyer family to have the shutters closed on a warm spring day?

I don't know. Maybe there is enough history to go around.

With your views of the park, she said. Not to look out? Why?

I come out to the park. As now. Must I defend myself? We've lived here all our lives, my brother and I. We do not neglect the park.

Good. In fact your Central Park is what drew me to New York, you know.

Oh, I said, I thought it was me.

Yes, that is what I am doing here besides meeting with strange men. She laughed. Walking in Central Park.

At that moment I wanted to touch her face. Her voice was in the alto register—a smoker's voice. When she had taken my arm, from the feel of her sleeve on my wrist—the material might have been corduroy—I had the impression of a woman in her late thirties, early forties. As we had walked across Fifth Avenue I thought her shoes might be what were called sensible, just from the sound of the heels hitting the ground, though I was no longer as confident of my deductions as I had once been.

I asked her what she hoped to find in the park. Parks are dull places, I said. Of course you can get murdered here at night, I said, but other than that it is very dull. Just the usual joggers, lovers, and nannies with baby carriages. In the winter everyone ice skates.

The nannies as well?

They are the best skaters.

So we had a rhythm going, making the kind of conversation that brings out one's competitive intelligence—at least it did mine. Or was it simply flirtation? How refreshing this was. I had a certain class. As if I had been flipped to a different side of myself.

Jacqueline Roux could laugh without losing her train of thought. No, she said, despite what you say your Central Park is different from any other park I have walked through in my life. Why do I feel that? Because it is so organized, so planned? A geometrical construction with such rigid borders—a cathedral of nature. No, I'm not sure. Do you know there are places in the park where I have had an awful feeling? Just for a moment or two yesterday in the late afternoon with its shadows, and the tall buildings surrounding on every side—nearby, and in the distance—I had the illusion that the park was too low!

Too low?

Yes, right where I was standing and everywhere I looked! It had rained and the grass was wet after the rain, and I for a moment recognized what I had not before seen, that the Central Park was sunken at the bottom of the city. And with its ponds and pools and lakes as if, you know, it is slowly sinking? That was my awful feeling. As if this is a sunken park, a sunken cathedral of nature inside a risen city.

How she could go on! Yet I was enchanted by the intensity of her conversation—so poetic, so philosophical, so French, for all I knew. But at the same time it was all too fanciful for me. Good Lord—to look for the meaning of Central Park? It was always across the street when I opened my door—something there, something fixed and unchanging and requiring no interpretation. I told her that. But in reacting to her idea I was yoked into an opinion of my own that was certainly a degree up from my nonthinking life.

I am relieved you know you suffered an illusion, I said.

It is too crazy, I grant you. I go back to my first impression—the design, made by artisans with picks and shovels, and so my thought is everyone's first thought—it is simply a work of art constructed from nature. Well that may have been only the intention of the designers.

Only the intention? I said. Is that not enough?

But to me it suggests what they may not have intended— a foretelling—this sequestered square of nature created for the time coming of the end of nature.

They built this park in the nineteenth century, I said. Before the city was there to surround it. Nature was everywhere, who would have thought about it coming to an end?

Nobody, she said. I have been shown the underground silos in South Dakota where the missiles wait and twenty-four hours a day the military sit at their consoles ready to turn the key in the box. The people who made this park didn't think about that either.

AND SO WE CHATTED away at what I realized was a level normal to her. How remarkable to be sitting there, as if at a sidewalk café in Paris, in conversation with a Frenchwoman with an alluring smoky voice. It was no small matter to me that she deemed me worthy of her thoughts. I said: You are looking for the secret. I don't think you have it yet.

Maybe not, she said.

I was glad she wasn't trying out her ideas on Langley—he wouldn't have had the patience, he might even have been rude. But I loved hearing her talk, never mind that she had bizarre theories—Central Park was sinking, shutters were un-American—her passionate engagement with her ideas was a revelation to me. Jacqueline Roux had been all over the world.

She was a published writer. I imagined how thrilling it must be living such a life, going around the world and making up things about it.

AND THEN IT was time to go.

Are you walking back? she said. I will walk with you.

We left the park and crossed Fifth Avenue, her arm in mine. In front of the house, I felt emboldened. Would you like to see the inside? I said. It is an attraction greater even than the Empire State Building.

Ah no, *merci,* I have appointments. But sometime, yes.

I said, Just let me get an idea of you. May I?

She had thick wavy hair cut short. A broad forehead, rounded cheekbones, a straight nose. A slight fullness under the chin. She wore glasses with wire frames. She wore no makeup. I did not think I should touch the lips.

I asked her if she was married.

No more, she said. It made no sense.

Children?

I have a son in Paris. In secondary school. So now you are interviewing me? She laughed.

She would be back in New York in a few weeks. We will have a coffee, she said.

I have no phone, I said. If I'm not in the park please knock on the door. I'm usually home. If I don't hear from you I'll try to get run over and there you will be.

I felt her looking at me. I hoped she was smiling.

Okay, Mr. Homer, she said, shaking my hand. Until we meet again.

WHEN LANGLEY RETURNED I told him about Jacqueline Roux. Another damn reporter, he said.

Not exactly a reporter, I said. A writer. A French lady writer.

I didn't know it had got as far as the European papers. What were you, her man-in-the-street interview?

It wasn't like that. We had some serious conversation. I invited her in and she refused. What reporter would do that?

It was hard trying to explain to Langley: this was another mind—not his, not mine.

She is a woman out in the world, I said. I was very impressed.

Apparently so.

She is divorced. Doesn't believe in marriage. A son in school.

Homer, you have always been susceptible to the ladies, do you know that?

I want to get a haircut. And maybe a new suit in one of those discount places. And I need to eat more. I don't like being this thin, I said.

HOURS LATER LANGLEY found me at the piano. She helped you across the street? he said.

Yes, and a lucky thing, I said.

Are you all right? It's not like you to misread traffic.

Ever since they made Fifth Avenue one-way is the problem, I said. It's a heavier, more congested sound with fewer gaps and I just have to get used to it.

Not like you at all, my brother said and left the room.

NATURALLY I WAS NOT able to hide my hearing problem from Langley—he had picked up on it almost immediately. I didn't say anything about it, I did not complain or even mention it, nor did he. It just became an unspoken understanding, an issue too fraught with anguish to speak about. If Langley had any instinct to attend to this matter it was not going to be as one of his cockamamie medical inspirations. I had been blind so long that his orange regimen and his theory of replenished cones and rods from vitamins and tactile training—well it was all in the nature of his self-expression and I wonder now if he ever meant it as anything more than a what-have-we-got-to-lose sort of impulse, or if it was more a manifestation of love for his brother than any conviction that some good would come of it. But maybe I misjudge him. With my hearing beginning to go, he of course didn't suggest that we see a doctor and I for myself knew that it would do no good, no more than a visit to the ophthalmologist had done years before. I had my own medical theories, perhaps this was a disposition given to the progeny of a doctor, but I believed my eyes and ears were in some intimate nervous association, they were analogous parts of a sensory system in which everything connected with everything else, and so

I knew what had been the fate of my vision would be the same for my hearing. With no sense of self-contradiction I also persuaded myself that the hearing loss would stabilize long before it was gone completely. I resolved to be hopeful and of good cheer and in this frame of mind waited for the return of Jacqueline Roux. I practiced some of my best pieces with the vague idea that I would somehow get to play for her. Langley quietly studied the books in our father's medical library—books probably outmoded in many ways given their age—but he did one day hold a small piece of metal against my head just behind the ear to see my reaction when he asked if there was any difference—pressing it to the bone behind the ear and then releasing it, and then holding it there again. I said no and that was the end of that modest experiment.

WHEN MONTHS WENT by and I did not hear from Jacqueline Roux, I began to think of her as an exotic accident, in the same sense that bird-watchers whom in past years I've chatted with in the park have informed me that birds discovered out of their normal range—a tropical specie for instance ending up, say, on a beach in North America—are called "accidentals." So perhaps Jacqueline Roux was a French accidental who happened to land on the sidewalk in front of our house for a rare one-time-only sighting.

I couldn't avoid feeling let down. I went over our conversation that day in the park and wondered if, in some cunning professional writer's way, she had led me on, and that I would be portrayed in her French newspaper as a total idiot. Perhaps I had been so grateful to be treated like a normal person that I had been overly enthralled with her. As time passed, and Langley and I became increasingly occupied with the war being waged against us by just about everyone, she, Jacqueline, began to figure in my mind as someone with flighty foreign ideas who had no place in our embattled world. The haircuts I got and the new suit of clothes I had bought in anticipation of her return were like any other played-out fantasies of mine. How pathetic—that I would think there was any possibility in my disabled life for a normal relationship outside of the Collyer house.

I was so hurt with disappointment that I could no longer think happily of Jacqueline Roux. There were mental shutters too and mine were closed tight as I turned back to what I could rely on, the filial bond.

AT THIS TIME MY brother was also down in the dumps. Only something as decisive as paying off a mortgage could have put him there. Whereas I was relieved that we no longer had to worry about losing our home, he felt amortization, militarily, as a defeat. I had thought his aplomb in dealing with the bank was praiseworthy, but he could think only of the end result: the money was gone. And so he was depressed and not very good company. The daily papers went unread. He would come back from his nighttime salvage operations empty-handed.

I didn't know what to do about this turn of events. I claimed, by way of cheering him up, that I thought my hearing was better—a lie. The portable radio by my bedside had stopped working, as well it might have at its advanced age—it was one of those heavy early portables with a handle for carrying that had been a great technical advance in radios fifty years before when it was imagined that a beach or a lawn were ideal places to hear the news. Can you replace this? I asked, thinking it might get him out of the house on one of his expeditions. Nothing.

By a perverse bit of good fortune, though, a registered letter was delivered one morning from a law firm representing "Con Edison"—the new slick name of the Consolidated Edison Company that we thought appropriately confessional and self-defining. I wanted to express my gratitude to these people: as Langley read aloud this egregiously rude and menacing letter, I could sense him rising like a lion from its slumber. Can you believe this, Homer? Some wretched legal clerk daring to address the Collyers in this manner?

Our struggle with the utility had gone on for years given our practice of paying bills in a desultory way as a matter of principle, and now, with Langley's foglike gloom suddenly lifting I felt everything returning to normal. Pacing about and swearing his undying hatred for this electromonopoly, as he called it, he proceeded to mail back the letter with his grammatical corrections in a nice neat packet of several years' of unpaid bills, altogether weighing, he claimed, a good quarter of a pound. Homer, he would later tell me, I felt privileged to pay the postage.

Never again would we be subject to Con Edison's intimida-

tion because quite abruptly the lights went out. I knew this because I was waiting for the electric coffeemaker to finish its ritual when it gurgled, spat a blot of hot water in my face, and
died. We were liberated, though without light. Apparently
some dim rays came through the louvered shutters, but not
enough for Langley to find any candles. We had a goodly supply of candles of every shape and kind, from dinner-table candles to sacramental candles in glasses, but of course they were
under something, somewhere in the house, and though I could
blunder about more easily than Langley neither of us could
remember where to even begin looking, and so an investment
was required. He went out and bought marine lamps, wilder-
ness lamps, long-handled searchlights, propane lamps, mercury
lamps, hurricane lamps, pocket flashlights, high-intensity beam
lamps on poles, and for the upstairs hall with its clerestory window, a battery-powered sodium lamp which went on automati-
cally as daylight faded. He even dug up an old buzzing sunlamp
meant to tan the skin that we had once used to keep our
mother's plants alive, burning them to death in the process, so
all that remained of her beloved nursery were stacks of clay pots
and the soil they held.

When these lights were turned on all over the house, I imagined great looming shadows angled off in different directions,
some streaming along the floor and bouncing up against the
bales of newspapers, others shooting upward at the ceiling to il-
luminate each drop of a particular leak. Not much had changed
as far as I was concerned, and I was diplomatic enough not to
ask Langley the initial cost of our investment in independent

power—to say nothing of the ongoing expense of battery replacements. The key thing here was our self-reliance and I was just as happy that we hadn't found the candles, which, what with one thing or another in our congested rooms, would no doubt have set something on fire—the piles of mattresses, the bundles of newsprint, the stacks of wooden crates my oranges came in, the old hanging tapestries, spillages of books, dust bunnies, the congealed puddle of oil under the Model T, God knows what—and brought us a return visit of the firemen with their rampant hoses.

THEN, AS IF INSPIRED by the malevolent electric company, the city turned off our water. Langley greeted this setback with relish. And I found myself participating with a kind of grim joy in the system we set up to provide ourselves with water. The hydrant at the curb was of no use—you could not circumspectly wrestle with a hydrant. What a psychological boost for me, then, to be working with my brother, a co-conspirator, as just before dawn every other morning or so we set out with two baby carriages in tandem, his with a ten-gallon milk can long since acquired with the idea that it might someday prove useful, and I with a couple of segmented crates filled with empty milk bottles gathered from our stoop when milk was delivered each morning to one's door with two or three inches of cream in the neck of the bottle.

A few blocks north of us there was an old water post from the days when water was made available for horses. The water post, a heavy-gauge faucet built into a low concave stone wall whose base was a cement trough, stood at the curb. Langley jammed the carriage up against the trough and positioned the milk can at a tilt under the faucet so that he wouldn't have to lift it out of the carriage. When the can was full, we filled each of the bottles and capped it with aluminum foil. The trip back was the difficult part, water weighing a lot more than I would have thought. To avoid the curbs at the ends of each block we went along in the street. There were no cars at this hour. I brought up the rear of our procession by keeping the folded carriage hood in touch with Langley's back. I think we both enjoyed a kind of boyish excitement there in the first light of morning, when no-body was abroad in the land except us and the freshness of the air was carried on a soft breeze redolent of a countryside, as if we were not pushing our carriages down Fifth Avenue, but along a back road.

We brought home our contraband through the basement door under the front steps. We would have enough water for drinking, and all our meals thenceforth would be on paper plates and with throwaway plastic utensils, though we didn't ex-actly throw them away, but water for commode flushing and for bathing was another matter. It was the ground-floor guest bath-room that we would try to keep functioning, which was just as well, as the upstairs bathrooms had long since served also as storage areas. But sponge baths were the order of the day and after a couple of weeks of turning ourselves into water carriers, the sense of triumph, of having put one over on the city, had given way to the hard realities of our situation. Of course there was an ordinary drinking fountain not far into the park across from our house and we used that to fill our thermoses and army canteens, though sometimes as the weather grew warmer we had to wait our turn as flocks of children with a perverse interest in water fountains pretended to be thirsty.

I DON'T KNOW IF any of the children who took to throwing stones at our shuttered windows were the same who had seen us come for water in the park. Most likely the word had spread. Children are the carriers of unholy superstition, and in the minds of the juvenile delinquents who'd begun to pelt our house Langley and I were not the eccentric recluses of a once well-to-do family as described in the press: we had metamorphosed, we were the ghosts who haunted the house we had once lived in. Not able to see myself or hear my own footsteps, I was coming around to the same idea.

At unpredictable times through the summer the assault would begin, the operation planned and the ordnance collected beforehand, because the clunks and thwacks and thuds came as a barrage. I could feel them. Sometimes I could hear the bel canto cries. I figured their ages to be from six to twelve. The first few times, Langley made the mistake of going out on the stoop and shaking his fist. The children scattered with screams of delight. So of course the next time there were even more of them and more rocks flew.

We had no thought of calling the police, nor did they of

their own volition ever appear. We settled back and endured these sorties as one would wait out summer showers. So now, it's even their children, Langley said, having assumed the little beasts lived in the surrounding houses and might have been inspired by their parents' opinion of us. I said my understanding of people of the class of our nearest neighbors was that they were not given to breeding. I said I thought it was a wider recruitment and the children's staging area was probably the park. When one day the rocks seemed to have a heftier impact, and I heard a shout in a deeper post-pubescent register, Langley lifted one of the shutter slats, peered out, and informed me that some of them were easily teenagers. So you are right, Homer, this may be citywide, and we have the rare privilege of an advanced look at the replacement citizenry for the millennium.

Langley began to think of a military action in response. He had collected a few pistols over the years and decided to take one and stand on the steps and wave it at the hoodlums to see what would happen. Of course it is not loaded, he said. I said he could do that—menace children with a deadly weapon—and that I would be happy to visit him in prison if I could find a way to get there. I was not inclined to fret over these stone throwers. The shutters had been well pocked and some of the brownstone frontage had been chipped but I knew the children would vanish when the weather grew cold, as they did, it was strictly a summer sport, and soon enough the thuds of rocks against the shutters were replaced by autumnal winds blowing through them and shaking our windows.

———

BUT ONE NIGHT SOMETHING Langley had said came back to
me as I tried to sleep. He said everything alive was at war. I
wondered if the diminution of my senses, even as I was terrified
of an enlarging consciousness slowly displacing the world outside my mind—if it was possible that I was becoming progres-
sively unaware of the truth of our situation, the magnitude of it,
protected in my insensitivity from the worst of its sights and
sounds. As I reflected, the stoning of our house by children,
rather than being an episode incidental to our major concerns—
our increasing isolation, losing by our own doing or the doing of
others the ordinary services of an urban civilization, no running
water, I mean, no gas, no electricity—and finding ourselves in a
circle of animosity rippling outward from our neighbors to
creditors, to the press, to the municipality, and, finally, to the
future—for that was what these children were—rather than
being of minor significance, well, that was the most devastating
blow of all. For what could be more terrible than being turned
into a mythic joke? How could we cope, once dead and gone,
with no one available to reclaim our history? My brother and I
were going down and he, lung-shot and half insane, knew that
better than I. Our every act of opposition and assertion of our
self-reliance, every instance of our creativity and resolute expression of our principles was in service of our ruination. And
he, apart from all that, had as his burden the care of an increasingly disabled brother. I will not criticize him then for the paranoia of that winter when he began to devise from the hoarded

materials of our life in this house—as if everything here had been amassed in response to a prophetic intelligence—the means of our last stand.

In the old days there was another poet he liked to quote: "I'm me, and what the hell can I do about it! . . . I, the solemn investigator of useless things."

MY OWN RESPONSE has been to press on with my daily writing. I am Homer Collyer and Jacqueline Roux is my muse. Though in my weakened state I am not sure if she ever returned as she said she would, or if I only needed the thought of her to begin this writing, a project comparable in its overreaching to Langley's newspaper. At this point I can't be sure of anything— what I imagine, what I recall—but she did come back, I'm almost sure of that, or let us say she did, and that I met her at the front door, having been groomed and turned out in some reasonable state by my understanding brother. Sitting in the chill of this house, I feel the warmth of a hotel lounge. Jacqueline and I have had dinner. There is a fireplace, arrangements of upholstered armchairs, small low tables for drinks, and a pianist playing standards. I remember this one from the time of our tea dances: "Strangers in the Night." I can tell from the stiffness of the playing that this is a classically trained pianist trying to make a living. Jacqueline and I laugh at the chosen song—the lyrics describing strangers exchanging glances, which is not possible between us, and ending up as lovers for life. That too is funny though in a way to stifle the laughter in my throat.

Then, on my second glass of the best wine I have ever tasted, I am impelled to sit at the piano after the hired help has withdrawn. I play Chopin, the Prelude in C-sharp Minor, because it is a slow chord-heavy piece that I can be reasonably sure of, not being able to hear it very well. Then I make the mistake of going into "Jesu, Joy of Man's Desiring," which requires a digitally meandering right hand: a mistake, because I understand from the touch on my shoulder—this is the lounge pianist stopping me—that I'm doing the sequence as Bach wrote it but I have started off on the wrong piano key. It is like a mockery of Bach. I am corrected and finish capably enough, but am led back to Jacqueline in total humiliation that I try to dissemble by laughing. What wine will do!

In her room I confess to my misery, a blind man going deaf.

A generous conversation ensues—practical, as if this is a problem to be solved. Why not write, then, she says. There is music in words, and it can be heard you know, by thinking.

I am not persuaded.

You understand, Mr. Homer? You think a word and you can hear its sound. I am telling you what I know—words have music and if you are a musician you will write to hear them.

The thought of life without my music is intolerable to me. I stand and pace. I blunder about and something goes over, a standing lamp. A bulb bursts. Jacqueline has my arm and sits me down on the bed. She sits beside me and takes my hand.

I say to her, Perhaps your French has music and so you think all language is musical. I do not hear music in my speech.

No, you are wrong.

And I have nothing to say. Given who I am what is there to write about?

Of course, your life, she says. Exactly who you are. Your life across from the park. Your history deserving of the black shutters. Your house that is a greater attraction than the Empire State Building.

And that is so sweetly and intimately funny that I cannot maintain my despair. It is overrun and we are laughing.

She allowed me to remove her glasses. And then the shivers of recognition as we lay together. This woman whom I barely knew. Who were we? Blindness and deafness was the world, there being nothing outside us. I don't remember the sex. I felt her heart beating. I remember her tears under our kisses. I remember holding her in my arms and absolving God of meaninglessness.

I AM GRATEFUL THAT Langley from the very beginning encouraged me to write in lieu of my music. Did he receive his instructions from Jacqueline Roux? Or do I only imagine a conversation in which he was uncharacteristically respectful and submissive as she outlined the new plan for my life? The fact is, Langley has made it his mission to keep me going. At one point my typewriter broke down and he took it to a repair shop on Fulton Street. But then I had to wait two weeks for the repair to be done, so he saw to it that I would have another Braille machine—two, in fact: a Hammond and an Underwood and thus I have been able to continue. With the three machines set up on this table, and reams of paper in a crate on the floor beside me, I am endowed. It is she for whom I write. My muse. If she does not come back, if I never see her again, I have her in my contemplation. But she has promised to read what I've written. She will have to forgive the misspellings and the grammatical errors and the typing errors. I write in Braille and it is supposed to come out in English.

I have been at it for some time now. I have no clear sense of how long. I sense the passage of time as a spatial thing, as Langley's voice has become fainter and fainter, as if he has walked off down a long road, or is falling away in space, or as if some other sound that I can't hear, a waterfall, has washed away his words. For a while I could still hear my brother as he shouted in my ear. At that time he devised a set of signals: he touches me once, twice, three times on the arm to mean he's brought me something to eat, or that it is time to go to bed, or other such basic matters of daily life. But more complicated messages are communicated by his putting my index finger on the Braille keys and spelling out the words. To do this, he had to learn Braille himself, which he did quite efficiently. In this way I get what news there is, briefly, as in a headline.

But for a while now, I have lived in total silence, and so when he approaches and taps me on the arm I sometimes start, for I think of him always at a distance, someone small and far away, when suddenly he is standing here, loomed up like an apparition. It is almost as if the reality is his distance from me and the illusion is his presence.

Writing happens to coincide with my compensatory desire to

stay alive. So I have kept busy in my own way while my brother goes about reconstructing the found materials of the house into an infernal machine. I have used the word *paranoia* to describe what he has done with the accumulations of decades. But in fact, almost with the first easing of the weather, he tells me a prowler did try to get through the back door at night. On another occasion he signaled that he heard someone moving about on the roof. I supposed we could anticipate more of the same: several of the newspapers from the very beginning of their stories about us had suggested that the Collyers, distrustful of banks, keep enormous amounts of cash stashed away. And for those street people and squatters who don't read the papers, our dark and decaying building is an open invitation.

A COMPLICATION HAS arisen. Langley's defensive strategy has made it unwise if not impossible for me to try to get around the house. For all practical purposes I am imprisoned. I am situated now just inside the doors of the drawing room with a single path to the bath under the stairs. Langley is also constrained. He has established himself in the kitchen with access in and out of the house through the back door to the garden. The front hall is completely blocked with boxes of books stacked to the ceiling. A narrow passageway between bales of newspaper and overhanging garden tools—shovels, rakes, a power drill, a wheelbarrow, all strung overhead by wire and rope from spikes he's hammered into the walls—leads from his kitchen outpost to my enclave. He brings me my meals down this tunneled passageway. He tells me he navigates by flashlight over the trapwires strung at ankle level from wall to wall.

My bed is a mattress on the floor beside my typing table. I also have a small transistor radio that I hold up to my ear in hopes of hearing something sometime. I know it is spring only from the mildness of the atmosphere and because I no longer have to wear the heavy sweaters of winter or cower under the bedclothes at night. Langley's bedroom is the kitchen and he sleeps, when he does, on the big table that once received our gangster friend Vincent.

My brother has taken pains to describe the snares and traps in the other rooms of the house. He is very proud of what he has done. Sometimes he puts my finger on the Braille keys for hours it seems like. Upstairs, he has so piled things up in pyramidal fashion that the least nudge of any one thing—rubber tires, an iron pressure cooker, dressmaker's dummies, empty bureau drawers, beer kegs, flowerpots—I almost take pleasure from visualizing the possibilities—and the whole assemblage will fall on the interloper, the mythical trespasser, the object of Langley's stratagems. Each room has its own punishing design of our things. Washboards greased with soap are laid on the floor for the unwary to step on. He is constantly busy working to improve the balance of the weights, and the snares and traps until he is sure they are perfect. One of his problems is the rats that have now come out of the walls. They pass through here at my feet regularly. He is at war with them. He bashes them with a shovel or takes up his old army rifle from the mantel and clubs them. I sometimes think I can hear something of what's going on. Once or twice a rat has fallen prey to his traps. For every dead rat he draws an invisible notch on my arm.

WITHAL, MY SENSE is of an end to this life. I remember our house as it was in our childhood: a glorious elegance prevailed, calming and festive at the same time. Life flowed through the rooms unencumbered by fear. We boys chased each other up and down the stairs and in and out of the rooms. We teased the servants and were teased by them. We marveled at our father's jarred specimens. As little boys we sat on the thick rugs and pushed our toy cars along the patterns. I took my piano lessons in the music room. We peeked from the hall at our parents' resplendent, candlelit dinner parties. My brother and I could run out the front door and down the steps and across to the park as if it was ours, as if home and park, both lit by the sun, were one and the same.

And when I lost my sight he read to me.

There are moments when I cannot bear this unremitting consciousness. It knows only itself. The images of things are not the things in themselves. Awake, I am in a continuum with my dreams. I feel my typewriters, my table, my chair to have that assurance of a solid world, where things take up space, where there is not the endless emptiness of insubstantial thought that leads to nowhere but itself. My memories pale as I prevail upon them again and again. They become more and more ghostly. I fear nothing so much as losing them altogether and having only my blank endless mind to live in. If I could go crazy, if I could will that on myself, I might not know how badly off I am, how awful is this awareness that is irremediably aware of itself. With only the touch of my brother's hand to know that I am not alone.

JACQUELINE, FOR HOW many days have I been without food. There was a crash, the whole house shook. Where is Langley? Where is my brother?

CITY OF GOD

E. L. Doctorow

'Alchemical writing . . . Exhilarating'
Daily Telegraph

'A heavy brass cross is stolen from St Timothy's Episcopal
Church in New York and discovered on the roof of the Synagogue
of Evolutionary Judaism. The crime, whose symbolism is
intriguing, brings together the sceptical Reverend Thomas
Pemberton and reformist Rabbi Sarah Blumethall. They turn
"divinity detectives", contemplating the case for God and religion
amid the decay of a city and a world . . . [this] is a novel bright
with invention, luminous with language . . . images flutter down
like sycamore leaves . . . the sheer linguistic élan of *City of God*
is both a constant pleasure and an indication of the resources
humankind can still pitch against the evidence for despair'
Independent

ABACUS
978-0-349-11352-4

SWEET LAND STORIES

E. L. Doctorow

'Beautifully written, meticulously plotted, scrupulously imagined'
New York Times Book Review

These dazzling short works are crafted with all the weight and
resonance of the novels for which E. L. Doctorow is famous.
You will find yourself set down set down in a mysterious redbrick
house in rural Illinois ('A House on the Plains'), working things
out with a baby-kidnapping couple in California ('Baby Wilson'),
living on a religious-cult commune in Kansas ('Walter John
Harmon'), sharing the heartrending cross-country journey of a
young woman navigating her way through three bad marriages
('Jolene: A Life'), and witnessing an FBI special agent at a
personal crossroads while he investigates a grave breach of
White House Security ('Child, Dead, in the Rose Garden').
Comprised in a variety of moods and voices, these remarkable
portrayals of the American spiritual landscape show
a modern master at the height of powers.

ABACUS
978-0-349-12019-5

THE MARCH

E. L. Doctorow

'Enormously subtle . . . A stunning achievement'
Independent on Sunday

In 1864 Union General William Sherman burned Atlanta
and marched his sixty thousand troops east, through Georgia
to the sea, and then up into the Carolinas. The army fought off
Confederate forces and lived off the land, pillaging the southern
plantations, taking cattle and crops for their own, demolishing
cities and accumulating a borne-along population of freed blacks
and white refugees until all that remained was the dangerous
transient life of the uprooted, the dispossessed and the triumphant.
Only a master novelist could so powerfully and compassionately
render the lives of those who marched.

'Doctorow raises evocation to an art-form in itself,
allowing the experience of war, of war in general,
to be revisited in all its intensity'
Sunday Times

ABACUS
978-0-349-11959-5

Now you can order superb titles directly from Abacus

☐ City of God	E. L. Doctorow	£9.99
☐ Sweet Land Stories	E. L. Doctorow	£7.99
☐ The March	E. L. Doctorow	£8.99

The prices shown above are correct at time of going to press. However, the publishers reserve the right to increase prices on covers from those previously advertised, without further notice.

───────────────── (ABACUS) ─────────────────

Please allow for postage and packing: **Free UK delivery.**
Europe: add 25% of retail price; Rest of World: 45% of retail price.

To order any of the above or any other Abacus titles, please call our credit card orderline or fill in this coupon and send/fax it to:

Abacus, PO Box 121, Kettering, Northants NN14 4ZQ
Fax: 01832 733076   Tel: 01832 737526
Email: aspenhouse@FSBDial.co.uk

☐ I enclose a UK bank cheque made payable to Abacus for £
☐ Please charge £   to my Visa/Delta/Maestro

☐☐☐☐☐☐☐☐☐☐☐☐☐☐☐☐☐☐☐

Expiry Date ☐☐☐☐   Maestro Issue No. ☐☐

NAME (BLOCK LETTERS please) ....
ADDRESS ....
....
....
Postcode .... Telephone ....
Signature ....

Please allow 28 days for delivery within the UK. Offer subject to price and availability.